Lana quickly discovered that activities with Mark were never routine.

As Lana uttered a grateful sigh, Furry spotted the stable too. Apparently ready for lunch and a nap, the horse gave a resounding snort and whinny, then seemingly sprouted wings and bolted forward with momentum just short of a Concorde's.

"Look at Miss West," Gary echoed behind her. "I wish I was riding Fury."

Fury? Her heart rose to her throat. She distinctly remembered Mark calling the brute Furry. And forget the well-worn path. Whether Furry or Fury, she and the steed left the others eating dust. As they flew across the field, her life ripped past in fast-forward.

The horse stopped before she did, and when woman and beast finally focused on each other, face-to-face, Lana found herself sprawled in his dinner on the floor of a stall.

Mark tore in behind her, waving his arms in panic. "Are you okay?" He stood over her, his face pale and pinched with concern. When he saw she had survived, his fear shifted gears to the familiar laugh that she'd grown to know too well.

"Put a muzzle on it," she said, rising to her feet and pulling straw from her hair. "Or you'll be eating this stuff."

She lifted an eyebrow, but the picture was too much even for her. Lana's laughter joined Mark's, and as she walked away from the stable, she had to admit her backside hurt much worse than her pride.

GAIL GAYMER MARTIN lives with her real-life hero and husband, Bob, in Lathrup Village, Michigan. Once a high school English and public speaking teacher, later a guidance counselor, Gail retired and taught English and speech at Davenport University. Now she is a full-time, award-winning, multipublished writer of romance fiction and the author of sixteen church resource books. Her first romance novel was published by Barbour in 1998, and in three years, God has blessed her with nearly twenty novel and novella sales.

Books by Gail Gaymer Martin

HEARTSONG PRESENTS
HP302—Seasons
HP330—Dreaming of Castles
HP462—Secrets Within

Over
Her Head

Gail Gaymer Martin

Heartsong Presents

To all my friends in American Christian Romance Writers.
Thanks for your friendship, laughter, and prayers.

A note from the author:
*I love to hear from my readers! You may correspond with me
by writing:*

> Gail Gaymer Martin
> Author Relations
> PO Box 719
> Uhrichsville, OH 44683

ISBN 1-58660-603-4

OVER HER HEAD

All Scripture quotations, unless otherwise indicated, are taken
from the HOLY BIBLE, NEW INTERNATIONAL VERSION®. NIV®. Copyright
© 1973, 1978, 1984 by International Bible Society. Used by per-
mission of Zondervan Publishing House. All rights reserved.

All of the characters and events in this book are fictitious. Any
resemblance to actual persons, living or dead, or to actual events
is purely coincidental.

Cover design by Ron Hall.

PRINTED IN THE U.S.A.

one

"What do you mean you brought home a man?"

Lana West peeked out the window at the attractive stranger on her front porch, then turned to her younger sister. "Why is he here?"

Barb gestured toward the lawn. "You've been complaining for weeks about the yard work."

Glancing at her wristwatch, Lana noted the time. "Now that I think of it, why are you here?"

"I'm running errands for my boss." Barb grinned. "Fridays are slow. He told me to take my time."

"Friday might be slow. . .but not you." Lana shook her head. "You're worse than a kid. I can't count the number of stray dogs and cats you've brought home. But this is ridiculous." Despite her astonishment, she chuckled. "This time you've brought home a stray man."

"He's not a stray. He needs a job."

"What happened to the Michigan Employment Agency?" Lana asked, half joking and half serious. Barb had always been the most soft-hearted person she'd known.

Frowning, Barb eyed her. "I hope you're kidding."

Lana sent her a halfhearted smile but didn't answer.

"You're always complaining about being too short to reach the upper limbs." Barb stepped toward the window. "Look at him. He's tall and strapping."

Lana had already noticed the man's build. She would have been blind not to, but she took another admiring peek anyway. "I'll grant you that," she conceded, amusement escaping her voice.

Barb lowered her arms in seeming disappointment. "I thought he'd be the answer to our prayers."

Looking at her sister's dejection and conceding Barb had been correct about her dislike for yard work, Lana admitted perhaps the tall, well-built handyman was God's answer to her prayers. The yard needed major spring pruning and trimming, and until school let out for the summer, Lana didn't have time to do anything but correct papers and write exams. Once school closed for the summer, she had a whole list of wonderful plans—things to do for herself. She could forget her students and class work and luxuriate in her own needs.

Finding a gracious way to admit defeat, Lana shrugged. "Since he's here, you might as well ask him to come around back, and I'll get him started. I know you need to get back to work."

"See," Barb said, "I knew you'd see my side of it." She tossed Lana a teasing grin and hurried out the door.

Watching her benevolent sister dart through the doorway, Lana breathed a deep sigh. If she didn't harness Barb's enthusiasm, her sister would force her into too many unwanted situations like she so often did. Barb had a knack for volunteering for anything while Lana liked to plan ahead—get organized and have a handle on things. Lana's counsel seemed to roll off her sister's back like rain off an umbrella.

Though Lana hated to admit it, she had a fault or two herself. Too often she plopped the burdens of the world on her own shoulders and forgot to let God carry some of the load. She prayed God would teach her how to let go and let God. . .or for that matter let anyone take charge except her. And patience. . . Lana pushed that fault from her mind. Going there would only depress her.

Pulling her thoughts together, she stepped through the side door into the attached garage and pulled out the equipment she figured the stranger would need. When she located all the yard tools, she strode into the backyard carrying a hedge trimmer, edger, and pruning shears.

Planning to supervise the stranger, Lana faltered when she faced the man directly. He had an air of authority that made her squirm, but drawing on her fortitude, she forged ahead. "My sister said you're looking for work."

He didn't respond, instead watching her with his arms folded across his ample chest and a mischievous twinkle in his crystal blue eyes.

His expression addled her. She found it unreadable—somewhere between perplexity and amusement. An uneasy feeling shuffled through her, and she hoped Barb hadn't hurried off to work too quickly. She might need defensive backup.

Trying to assume a look of control, she ignored his stare and motioned to the garage access door. "You'll find anything else you need in there," she said, dropping the pruning scissors and edger onto a garden bench. Feeling a sense of authority, she clung to the trimmer.

He gestured toward the bench. "Looks like you have about every tool a man would need right here."

His rich, clear voice surprised her. For someone who couldn't find a job, the man sounded educated. . .and articulate. Recognizing her uncharitable attitude, Lana cringed.

"So, what did you have in mind?" he asked, stepping toward her.

"If you look around," she said, clinging to the trimmer and motioning toward the tall shrubs while turning one hundred eighty degrees, "you'll see—"

As she swished past him, the man ducked and shot backward.

"Sorry," she said, embarrassed that she'd wielded the gas-powered trimmer like a machete. "You can see why I don't do this myself. I'm dangerous handling anything with a motor."

His eyes crinkled in a warm smile. "Yes, I see that." He grasped the trimmer handle. "Why don't you give me that weapon before you hurt one of us."

Lana relinquished the implement into his large hands. Undaunted, she led him around the yard, explaining what needed to be pruned and shaped, but each time she faced him squarely, his smiling eyes flustered her, and her pulse sputtered like the gas-driven trimmer.

Realizing her earlier fear had been foolish, Lana couldn't help but admire the man. His gentle spirit and good humor surprised her, coming from a person without a job. He commented with familiarity about the shrubs and grasped her instructions. While the yard tour preoccupied him, she used the time to quiet her revving heart.

"What do you think?" she asked, motioning to the work.

"I think I've got it," he said, giving her a polite nod that came close to a bow.

"I'll be inside if you have any questions."

Lana made her escape into the sanctuary of the house. What in the world had gotten into her? She felt wildly out of control, like a stampede pursued by experienced herdsmen.

Forcing herself to concentrate on her work, two hours passed before she heard a knock on the backdoor. When she answered, he stood outside, perspiration and dirt smudges sullying his good looks.

"I'm sorry," she said, thinking of her manners. "Here I am sitting in air-conditioning, and I didn't give a thought to offering you something cold. I can't believe May has had such high temperatures. Would you like something to drink?" She looked beyond his shoulder and surveyed the backyard. Already his work had created vast improvements in the landscaping.

"No, thanks. It's getting late. I'll have to come back and finish. Maybe tomorrow. It's time to call the dealer to see if my car's ready."

"The dealer?" Rattled, Lana played with the top button of

her knit top. "You mean you own a car?"

"Sure do. I dropped it off this morning for the six-month maintenance check-up."

No job and a sixth month check-up? "You mean it's a new car?" Her pitch hit the top of a piano scale. Embarrassed, she modulated her tone. "I had no idea."

"Why would you?" he asked. With a soft chuckle, he pushed the amber-colored hair from his forehead.

Struggling to make sense out of their conversation, Lana peered into his face and organized her thoughts. "I don't understand. My sister said you were—"

"A slight misunderstanding, I think." He rubbed the back of his neck. "I'm your new neighbor. . .temporary new neighbor." He wiped his fingers on his newly soiled trousers and stretched his arm toward her. "Mark Branson."

Humiliated, she stood dumb struck. "My temporary new neighbor?" Then, like a sleepwalker, she extended her arm. "I'm so sorry. I'm Lana West."

His handshake felt firm, and the amiable warmth rolled up her arm.

"It's okay," he said, his smile as caring as the Good Samaritan. "I just moved into town, and I'm staying with a long-time friend. Jim Spalinni."

She felt her mouth sag, and she snapped it closed. "You mean you're staying. . .there." She pointed to the neat brick ranch next door.

He grinned and nodded. "Until I get a place of my own. That's my next project."

"I have no idea how my sister let this happen." A headache stole up her neck and throbbed in her temples.

He shifted uneasily and tucked his soiled hands into his pockets. "To be honest, I didn't understand the mix-up at first either. When I sorted out what had happened, I hated to embarrass you." He released a good-natured laugh. "Anyway,

I had time to kill."

She circled two fingers along her aching forehead. "I don't understand. I gather my sister got confused somehow."

"Apparently." He appeared to cover an escaping chuckle. "When she pulled up, I recognized her as a neighbor and gave a wave."

Lana listened, confounded while he unraveled the mess-up.

"Your sister. . .what's her name?" Mark asked

"Barb," Lana answered, wanting to scream at her sister's ridiculous faux pas.

"Anyway," he continued, "Barb asked if she could help. I said, sure, thinking she recognized me. When she said, 'Climb in,' I didn't think twice. I didn't have to pay taxi fare."

Lana shook her head. "Why didn't you say something sooner? I feel like a fool."

His face filled with amusement. "I got a kick out of it. Figured it would make an amusing story." He gestured behind him toward the access door. "By the way, I put your tools back in the garage."

Tension rose up Lana's spine. "I'll wring Barb's neck when she gets home."

Grinning, he flexed his palm in protest. "Don't let me be the cause of sibling-cide."

She smiled back despite her irritation. "I believe that's fratricide." She swung around, looking for her purse. Paying him for the work seemed the least she could do.

His eyes leveled toward her mouth. "You should do that more often."

"What?"

"Smile. It looks nice on you."

A burning flush heated her cheeks. She never blushed, and the sensation left her feeling helpless. "Please come in for a minute," she said, opening the screen door.

He stepped inside, and she hurried to the kitchen table and

pulled a wallet from her bag. "Let me pay you. . .despite the mix-up."

He wove his fingers together behind him and backed away, shaking his head. "I haven't finished the job yet. At Branson's, we guarantee to please our customers."

She thrust the bills toward him. "No, please take the money. I'm serious."

"So am I. God tells us to treat our neighbors as we'd like to be treated. Maybe someday I'll need a favor, and you'll be waiting there with a willing smile like the one I just saw a second ago."

A favor? She didn't do favors. . .though she knew she should. Discomfort edged up her collar again, and she pulled on the neck of her blouse, hoping the motion might scare away her embarrassment. "You're a Christian? That's nice."

"Sure am," he said, a look of joy filling his face. "How about you?"

She nodded. "I was raised knowing Jesus, but I don't think I've gotten the Ten Commandments down as well as you have. I'm working on them."

Tender humor settled on his face. "We all are. How are you doing?"

"With the commandments?"

He nodded.

"I'm still struggling with the first one."

He ran his fingers through his hair and pushed back an unruly strand while sending a rich, warm laugh into the air. "Me too."

"I'm serious," she said. "Look at what you did today. I'm usually so busy with my own well-polished agenda, I don't notice other people's needs." She winced, wondering why she was confessing her sins so blatantly. "When I do notice, I'm usually tied up with my own plans." She shook her head. "See. That's just one of the sins I have to conquer."

"If I had time, I'd confess mine." He scanned the room and motioned behind her. "Could I use your telephone? I'll see if the car's ready."

"After you did my yard work, how could I refuse?" She gestured toward the wall phone. "If it's ready, I'll be happy to give you a ride to the dealer."

Mark grinned at the petite woman who demonstrated so much pluck—the woman who'd just mentioned she didn't do favors. "You're not trying to get off that easy, are you?"

A pink tinge rolled up her neck.

He grinned and headed for the telephone. She seemed a paradox—soft inside and hard on the outside like candy-coated chocolate or a child with a toy backhoe trying to move a mountain. Lana had marched him around the yard, instructing him about what he should prune and what he shouldn't. Tucking her short brown hair behind her ears, she'd eyed him with riveting gray eyes. She certainly had supervisory skills, but he liked that.

When she shoved the bills back into her wallet, she'd struggled to maintain a calm exterior, but her embarrassment colored her fair skin, giving her away. He had to chuckle, and though Mark felt a little guilty, he enjoyed seeing her a little tongue-tied and out-of-control.

He pulled the dealer's business card from his shirt pocket while he scanned the tidy, antique-filled kitchen. Though the cabinets and countertops were modern, one wall was covered with baskets, old wooden spoons discolored from age, and antique kitchen implements whose original uses he couldn't imagine—except for an old rug-beater that hung near the doorway.

"Nice place," he said, lifting the telephone and punching in the telephone number.

"Thanks," she said.

Before he connected with the dealer, Lana left the kitchen.

His inquiry was answered with speed, and when he hung up, he peeked into the living room, thinking he'd find her there. Instead, the room stood empty. Letting his gaze sweep the room, he enjoyed the cozy feeling. As if in welcome, an antique oak table held a floral bouquet, and near the door, vintage umbrellas with carved handles rested in an antique stand. Everything in place. Everything fitting—so much like the paradox herself.

Not wanting to wander farther, he retreated to the kitchen and called her name.

In a heartbeat, she came through the door. "Everything okay?"

"Someone will drive my car here, and I'll take him back. Thanks for letting me use your phone."

A warm smile curved her full lips. "You're very welcome. I'm really sorry for the confusion. But the more I think about it, I can't help but laugh." She lifted a finger and shook it in the air. "Wait until Barbara gets home."

"Should I hide the weapons?"

"No, I promise I'll be gentle. That's one commandment I've mastered."

Her smile wove through his chest, and Mark sent up a silent prayer. If God willed it, he wanted to get better acquainted with this spirited woman.

"But maybe you could. . ."

Her pause aroused his curiosity. "Could what?"

She'd lost her commanding presence and stood beside him obviously nervous.

"You could. . .drop by later just to make sure I don't do her harm. For dinner, maybe." Her lovely gray eyes widened as she waited.

Her discomfort assured him she'd never asked a man to dinner before, and he delighted in her innocence. "I think that can be arranged." He ran his fingers over his chin in playful thought. "Although you have to understand that one dinner isn't going to pay off this debt either."

"Okay," she said, grinning. "I still owe you."

He loved the idea, and after agreeing on a time for him to arrive for dinner, he stepped outside and calmed himself. Like a schoolboy tripping over his shoelaces, he tethered his excitement and forced himself to behave his age—a man pushing thirty—no matter how joyful he felt.

❧

When Barb walked in from work, Lana barraged her with questions like BB shot. "Why? How? What made you think. . . ?"

"I'm serious. I passed this guy with a poster that said, 'Looking for any kind of work,' and I felt guilty. We're Christians, and I knew we had yard work. . .so I backtracked."

"I'd say so," Lana said, finding her sister's story both amusing and outlandish.

Barb huffed. "When I swung around the block again, I didn't see the sign, but the same guy stood there in jeans and a T-shirt." She narrowed her eyes. "At least, I assumed he was the same guy who'd ditched his sign. I'd only been gone a minute."

Lana tried to tuck away the grin, but it rose on her face anyway. "Barb, where did you think he pitched the sign?"

"I didn't think."

"Precisely," Lana said, marking a victory into the air before teasing her sister some more. "But you're fortunate. I promised not to harm you." She warmed, remembering her conversation with Mark.

"Promised who?" A frown rested on Barb's face.

"Our handyman. . .our neighbor."

"Temporary neighbor." Barb said, her scowl shifting to a toothy grin. "Nice guy, isn't he?"

Trying to contain her chuckle, Lana folded her arms and nodded.

"What's the grin for?" her sister asked, suspicion edging her voice.

"He's sooo nice. . .I've invited him to dinner."

"Dinner?" Disappointment spread across her face. "I'm going out with friends tonight."

"Then, it's your loss," Lana shrugged, sending her sister the illusion of confidence, but a tremor of nervous energy rifled through her. Now she'd have to entertain the man alone.

"Apologize for me, will you?" Barb said as she scooted through the doorway.

"I've apologized for you numerous times," Lana said, staring at the empty doorway. Her response fell into the air. Apparently Barb didn't have time for more chitchat. She had plans.

And so did Lana. A dinner to make in less than an hour. . . by herself.

After she'd offered Mark the invitation, Lana had pondered what to serve. Not knowing his likes or dislikes, she'd settled on chicken. She didn't know anyone who didn't like fried chicken.

Scrounging through a folder of recipes, Lana found one a friend had given her. With flour and herbs blended in a shallow bowl, she added ground peanuts and used the mixture on the chicken with a milk and egg wash. Letting it stand for a few minutes was the secret.

She dashed between the kitchen and the small dining room, setting the table and keeping an eye on the food. When the doorbell rang, Lana had been so preoccupied she'd forgotten to be nervous.

Opening the door, she gave a quiet gasp. Mark looked wonderfully attractive in khaki trousers and an electric blue knit shirt, the color enhancing his light blue eyes. To her delight, he held a single yellow rosebud and a carton of ice cream.

"Dessert," he said.

"Which one?" she asked, hiding her smile.

"The ice cream. The flower is the centerpiece."

She loved his sense of humor and accepted both the gifts with a thank you. "Have a seat, and I'll be right back." She gestured toward the living room.

In the kitchen, she slid the dessert into the freezer—grateful for the contribution because all she had in the house were some store-bought cookies. Then she found a vase on an upper cabinet shelf and placed the flower in water. "Want a soda?" she called, opening the refrigerator door and scanning inside.

"Sounds great," he said so close to her ear that her heart rose to her throat.

Swallowing a scream, she spun toward him. "You scared me. I thought you were in the living room." Though the fried chicken sizzled in the skillet and sent out a delectable aroma, Lana inhaled an exotic scent like a rain forest blended with island spices. She looked into his eyes and seemed to sail away to a tranquil Caribbean lagoon. "You smell good," she said.

"Not as good as whatever's in that frying pan."

"It's chicken," she said. But the statement triggered a new thought, and she lowered her arms in frustration. "I forgot to bake the biscuits. It'll only take a minute." She snapped on the oven, then turned down the chicken and pan of rice. Again her delayed manners struck her. "Please get us some soda out of the refrigerator. You scared the thought right out of me."

With a good-natured nod, he opened the refrigerator and pulled out two cans. In a moment the biscuits were in the oven, and Mark handed her one of the sodas. She watched him swig from his can, and so she followed, feeling the cold effervescence cool her throat.

"Let's sit for a minute." She beckoned him into the living room and motioned him to an easy chair. "I'd like to hear more about you. Tell me why you moved to a small town like Holly."

He took another sip and rested the can on his knee. "A new job. I start next week."

"That's great. What do you do?" she asked, curious what type of business would entice a handsome young man to a rural town.

"I'm a youth director. I'll—"

"I work with kids too." She realized her voice lacked enthusiasm.

"Where do you work?" he asked.

"Holly High School. I'm a social studies teacher. Kids hate history. Sometimes I wish I'd never see another teenager."

His face twisted with concern, and she wished she'd closed her mouth.

"I don't mean that exactly," she corrected. "I suppose most of the time it's their foolish excuses for not doing their homework and their obvious disinterest in learning. Even the brightest ones want to take the easy way out of learning."

"I know," he said. "They can be a handful. . .but not all of them. And even the bad ones are redeemable with a little love and compassion."

His words hit her like a rock. She needed to talk to God about her attitude. "You're so much like my sister."

He leaned forward. "You mean bringing strangers home?"

"Maybe that too," she said, thinking of Barb and her stray animals. "You and my sister seem to be Good Samaritans."

He leaned back against the cushion and chuckled. "I suppose it's part of the job."

A vague notion rattled through her, and humiliation began to creep up her back. "Don't tell me you're a minister?"

"No. Not a minister." The same mischievous grin she saw that afternoon slipped onto his face.

"What then?" She closed her eyes and tethered her hands from covering her ears.

"I'm a church youth director. Almost as bad, isn't it?"

"Yes. . .I mean no. . .I mean. . ." As his words sank into her brain, Lana had another mortifying realization. "Don't tell me." Why hadn't it dawned on her before? "You're the new youth director at First Church of Holly."

"How did you guess?"

A frown stirred his face a heartbeat before the smoke detector let loose its shrill scream.

"The biscuits," Lana yelled, bounding toward the kitchen with Mark following on her heels.

Smoke rolled from the oven while she turned the knob to off and yanked open the door. Before she could ask Mark to dismantle the alarm, he'd anticipated the need and darted into the hallway.

The noise stopped, and Mark came back holding the battery. "Saved by a long arm. I also opened the side door."

"Thanks," she said, feeling defeated. She grabbed the potholders and pulled out the blackened biscuits. "Remember, I'm a teacher, not a chef."

"I can see that," he said with a chuckle, then looked into the frying pan. "No real harm. The chicken still looks and smells great.

She slid the baking tin into the sink, realizing she hadn't answered his earlier question before the alarm went off. She let the subject drop. If he didn't pursue it again, the answer would be her surprise.

In moments, they were seated at the table. Her golden brown chicken looked like a picture postcard, and to her relief, the rice pilaf had remained moist. Before dishing the salad, they bowed their heads, and Mark offered the blessing.

For once her organization and quick planning paid off. Mark took a second helping of everything, and despite the loss of the biscuits, her meal had turned out a success.

But as they talked, Mark's expression began to concern Lana. A look of discomfort had settled over him. He'd begun to rub his throat and seemed to have difficulty swallowing. His cough worried her more, and concern stabbed through her. Mark grasped the water glass and gulped.

Lana leaned forward, watching panic grow in his eye. "Is something wrong?"

"No. . .yes, it's my throat. I can't breathe."

"You look terrible," she said, being not only honest but concerned. She'd put nothing spicy on the food. Her mind ran over the list of ingredients, her own panic growing.

"There's only one thing I'm allergic to that bothers me like this. . .but—"

"What are you allergic to, Mark?" She held her breath, afraid to hear his answer.

"Peanuts, but I didn't—"

"Yes, you did."

"I did?" As his eyes widened the size of baseballs, his jaw dropped open.

If she could have commanded the floor to open, she would have. "I put ground peanuts in the chicken batter."

He rose like a bullet, sending the chair on a spiraling journey. "I have to get my medicine," he gasped, reaching the doorway before Lana could think.

"I'll come with you," Lana cried, following him outside. She cringed as she spouted her next thought. "You might need me to call an ambulance."

By the time she reached his front door, Mark had vanished. Her heart pounded with fear. "Where are you?" she yelled. The house had the same floor plan as hers, and she followed a noise to the kitchen.

Mark sat on a kitchen chair, an EpiPen stuck through his pant leg. He held the device in place for a few seconds, and afraid to speak, she waited until he withdrew the needle.

"What can I do?" she asked. "I'll drive you to the hospital or call an ambulance."

He concentrated on his leg, massaging the spot where he'd inserted the needle. Finally he lifted his head. "No. . .I'll be fine now."

"Are you sure? It's no trouble." Trouble. She'd caused him the trouble. "Where's Jim? Will he be home soon?"

A faint grin settled on his mouth. "Really. Don't worry. I'm fine."

"But I feel so responsible."

"You didn't know. I should have told you about the peanut allergy." He pinched his lips together and shook his head. "And I should have had the EpiPen with me. I'm supposed to carry it when I go out. . .but you only live next door and. . ."

Though he still looked flushed, she couldn't hold back a smile. "So, you're not perfect after all."

He chuckled at her comment. "I plead the Fifth."

She stood nearby, wondering what she should do. "We have ice cream for dessert. Do you want to come back and—"

"Thanks. No. We'd better call it a night. I'm fine, but I need to stay put and let the medication do its job."

"I'll wait with you." She pulled a chair out and sat down at the table.

He didn't argue, and they talked for a few moments, but she could see he was uncomfortable. "I suppose I should get going."

He nodded. "This takes awhile, but I'm okay. Really."

She rose and backed toward the doorway. "I'll let myself out. You take care, and I'll call you in the morning. Okay?"

"Sure. . .and thanks for the great. . .dinner."

Guilt crawled up her spine. She gave a wave and spun around, heading for the front door. Reality hit her like buck shot. She'd nearly killed the first man who'd appealed to her in a long, long time.

two

The next morning, Lana sat at the kitchen table, thinking about the horrible evening. She'd told Mark she would call him, but it was early and she thought, since she'd tried to kill him, he might still be in bed.

Being her neighbor made the matter worse. If Mark lived across town, she might see him only on Sundays at church, but now the incident would live in her memory every time she saw his face.

While Lana tucked her cotton robe around her and sipped her second coffee, Barb bounded into the room, fully dressed, and plopped onto a chair. "Hey, Sis, very attractive wrap you're wearing." Barb gave a chuckle and leaned back, eyeing her with a curious gaze.

Lana looked down at the bright yellow-and-orange robe with Flub-a-Dub on the front and smiled along with her. "I found this the other day. Remember when Mom was on one of her memorabilia kicks? The old Howdy Doody television show was celebrating some anniversary, I guess." She poked at the familiar puppet faces grinning from the cloth. "I look stupid, but I tossed my summer robe in the laundry. I ran across this in the things-we-should-throw-away closet."

"Well, between your 'Clarabell the Clown' hair and 'Howdy Doody' robe, you look just great."

"Thanks," Lana said, knowing she hadn't done anything to improve her looks since she'd crawled out of bed.

Barb glanced at her watch and bolted up. "Whoa! I have a dentist appointment in ten minutes. Where did the time go?" She darted away and returned with her shoulder bag.

"Could you toss in the newspaper before you leave?" Lana asked, rising and putting her cup into the sink.

Barb glanced at her wristwatch. "Sorry. I'm really running late." She hurried past Lana and out the side door to the garage. "No one will see you, and if they did," her voice rang with humor, "they wouldn't believe their eyes. They'd think it was an apparition."

Lana followed Barb into the garage and peeked outside toward the mailbox and newspaper holder at the curb. The street appeared empty. She gave one cautious look toward the Spalinni house. Nothing but silence. She ducked behind Barb's car as it backed out of the garage and followed it down the driveway, figuring that it would camouflage her from the view of one particular neighbor. Once she had the newspaper in her clutches, she'd dart back inside, undetected.

As Barb backed onto the road, Lana snatched the paper from the box and turned toward the garage. Her sister tooted a good-bye and headed down the street.

Not taking the time to wave, Lana bounded toward the safety of the house but panicked as she watched the garage door lower into place. "You hit the remote," she yelled, turning toward the road and trying to flag her sister. Why? Why? Why? She gaped at the empty street, realizing Barb had pushed the closure button out of habit.

Lana heard the garage door bump against the pavement, then gave another desperate look down the street just in time to see Barb's car round a corner and vanish from sight. Standing in the driveway, Lana closed her eyes in a silent prayer. *Please, Lord, work a miracle for me.*

Struck by a thought, Lana rushed into the backyard. Maybe she'd left the garage access door unlocked. The possibility seemed good since Mark had put the tools away for her.

When she turned the doorknob, she grimaced. The access door had been locked tight. Mark had done a top-notch job of safeguarding her lawn equipment.

Lana gaped downward at her garish bathrobe. Who would have thought she'd find herself locked outside in this ridiculous garb? Now what could she do?

She weighed her alternatives. Hiding in the backyard until Barb came home from the dentist didn't make much sense. Knowing Barb, she'd probably handle twenty other errands before trekking home. If the situation didn't seem so outlandish, Lana would have cried. But all she could do was gaze at her gaudy reflection in the window glass and laugh.

A small step ladder lay against the back of the garage. She remembered using it to fill the bird feeders, and with trepidation, she carried it to the lower windows to check the locks, but each one she tried was tightly fastened.

Peeking around the front of the house, she eyed the quiet street. One last hope sailed into her mind. The dining-room window. Dragging the ladder, she raced around the house and climbed the two steps to the window. Locked. Her shoulders slumped.

"Howdy, Doody." A friendly guffaw sounded behind her. She propped her body against the ladder to avoid tumbling to the ground. Looking over her shoulder, she saw Mark standing directly behind her with a five-star grin spread from ear to ear.

"Nice get-up," he observed.

"Thanks. I see you lived through the night," she replied, covering her mortification.

"No thanks to you." His voice lilted with humor. "But I do appreciate your efforts to make up for the damage." He chuckled once again. "Where'd you buy that charming outfit?"

Though she had a layer of pajamas beneath, Lana grabbed the neck of her robe and tugged it closed, feeling utterly mortified. "Don't ask. . .and don't say another word."

"Then I suppose you don't want my help either." His voice sang out with amusement. "I have a very tall ladder."

Struggling for courage, Lana gazed at him. "A real tall one?"

"Sure thing. It'll reach the second story." Mark playfully jiggled his eyebrows.

"That would be great. Thanks." She stepped to the ground, clinging to her colorful cover-up.

"Anything open up there?" he asked.

"The bathroom window maybe. While you check, I'll hide in the backyard."

"Right," he said with a straight face.

She took off on a run, his laughter following her around the corner of the house.

Lana waited in a lawn chair under the tree, and in a few minutes, the garage access door opened, and Mark appeared. "You can get in now, Miss Doody."

She rose from the chair like a marionette jerked into action and bolted past him into the house. "Thank you," she called.

Tucked between his distant laughter, she heard his voice. "Don't mention it. . .but you can be sure I will. You owe me now. No question."

☙

Lana and Barb strode into church and slid into a center pew. Lana nodded to a couple students she knew from the school. Sometimes she was shocked to see them in church after watching their behavior in class. She wished she knew how to make a difference in their lives.

The opening music ended, and the congregation rose to join in the first hymn. She scanned the worship area, wondering where Mark was. Saturday, after she'd dressed and calmed down, she'd called him, but no one had answered. She guessed he'd been at the church all day. . .which was probably for the best. Her behavior seemed questionable around him. Never having told him she was a member there, she couldn't wait to see his surprise.

Opening the hymn book, Lana read the familiar words. She

loved the music and prayers but often left church with a shard of guilt pressing against her like a minute sliver impossible to extract. She knew the commandments, and she'd read the Bible. Parts, anyway. She just didn't seem to follow it the way a Christian should. Granted, all of God's children sinned, but her sins started with a capital S. At least, that's how she felt. Barb inevitably chattered all the way home about the wonderful message, seeming to feel sinless. Lana knew better.

This morning the pastor rose. "Today we'll focus on Psalm 46," Pastor Phil said, allowing people time to open their Bibles. "God is our refuge and strength, an ever-present help in trouble. Therefore we will not fear, though the earth give way and the mountains fall into the heart of the sea, though its waters roar and foam. . . ."

Lana's mind drifted, and the source of her guilt edged into her consciousness. Her age-old problem. She tried to be her own refuge and strength. Her own help in time of trouble. And she rarely felt eager to help anyone else. What would life be like if she were like her sister, always helping the needy and concerned about others. . .like stray—'?

" 'Be still, and know that I am God.' " Pastor Phil's words struck Lana's ears like a jackhammer, as if God Himself had pinned her to the chair. She ruefully recognized that she wasn't still very often. She preferred to direct everyone else's traffic as well as her own. She needed to remember those words. "Be still, and know that I am God," she whispered.

Scowling, Barb hissed in her ear. "Shush. You may think you're God, but don't tell everyone around you."

Lana's heart jolted. Had she said the words aloud? She slid lower in the pew and kept her lips sealed.

Near the end of the service, Lana's distracted thoughts settled on her very empty stomach. Fearing she'd be late for church, she had neglected to eat breakfast. To add to her emptiness, Mark seemed nowhere in sight.

But Pastor Phil came forward, as if God considered Lana's concern, and addressed the congregation. "This morning I'm happy to introduce you to our long-awaited youth director, Mark Branson. Mark is ready and eager to begin working with our young people." He scanned the congregation, a look of apprehension on his face. "Mark?"

Lana's heart sank. Had Mark overslept or, worse yet, died during the night from her dinner?

The pastor's face brightened, and Mark came down the aisle from the back of the sanctuary. When he turned to face the congregation, Lana's heart tripped over itself. He looked terribly handsome in gray slacks and a navy blazer with a gray and navy tie against his white shirt—a dramatic contrast to the jeans and casual shirt he'd been wearing when she first met him.

"Thank you, Pastor Phil," he said, his eyes filled with plea-sure as he scanned the worshipers. "I'm looking forward to getting to know the young people of this congregation. Young people are filled with untapped energy and spirit. I think together we can build a strong youth organization here. I ask for your prayers as I begin my ministry."

The congregation applauded as Mark retreated down the aisle. After the final hymn, Lana worked her way toward the exit with Barb on her heels, both anxious to get some food. Before Lana reached the foyer, Mark's voice wrapped around her thoughts like waxed paper on a sandwich.

"If it isn't Miss Doody. Great to see you here. Where's your fancy costume?"

For the second time that morning, she felt pinned to the spot. "At home on a hook." She faced Mark's amused gaze which, at the moment, looked even more appealing than a honey-baked ham. "Surprised to see me?" she asked.

"I am. What are you doing here. . .besides worshiping, that is?"

"This is my church. I've been a member here for years."

He looked puzzled. "You never mentioned it."

"No. I would have except I had to answer my smoke alarm." She rolled her eyes. "You haven't forgotten, have you?"

"Now that I think about it, you did leave me hanging that day."

His taunting eyes ruffled her emotions again. "You mean choking. I tried calling yesterday afternoon to thank you again for opening my door."

He sent her a heartwarming grin. "Sorry I missed your call."

"I still feel badly about that dinner. You look great today," Lana said.

"Don't feel guilty. Like I said, I'm sorry I didn't mention my peanut allergy. You said dinner, so the problem hadn't entered my mind."

"I'll know next time." Uneasy, she focused on the beige tweed carpet.

"Next time? Now that sounds promising." He slid his hand into his jacket pocket. "Did you want to set a date?"

Her pulse kicked like a mule, and she raised her head, hoping she could hide her attraction. "I was speaking figuratively. Right now, I'm on my way to breakfast." She scanned the crowd looking for Barb. "But I've lost my sister, it seems."

"I'm sure she hasn't gone far." He gazed over the milling worshipers, then faced her again. "Breakfast? Sure that's a great offer." He pulled his hand from his pocket and ran it through his hair.

"Offer?" She laughed. "You mean you're coming along?"

"Why not? It sounds safe. No peanuts."

She rested her fingers on his arm. "Will you ever forgive me?"

"You were forgiven when I saw your horrified expression. No words needed."

No words needed. The Bible said God forgave like that. But the Bible also talked about repentance, and until she could lasso some patience and compassion, forgiveness seemed hopeless. "Let me find Barb," Lana said, distracted by her thoughts.

As she walked through the church's front door, Lana spotted her sister in a circle of friends.

"Do you mind if we skip breakfast?" Barb asked when Lana caught her attention. "Jenny invited me to her place for brunch."

"That's fine," Lana said, hoping she could come up with some interesting conversation at breakfast rather than revealing all her idiosyncrasies and flaws. She wished she were a woman worthy of spending time with a kindly, handsome youth director.

"Ready?" Mark asked, slipping behind her.

"Barb's going to brunch with friends," she said.

"No problem. Why not ride with me, and I'll bring you back for your car?"

She nodded and followed him to the parking lot, admitting his safety seemed more guaranteed in a restaurant than at her house. Between the burnt biscuits and peanut poisoning, she'd become a human danger zone.

✤

Mark placed his menu on the table and watched Lana peruse the breakfast choices. He'd never seen her in a dress before. Around the house she wore jeans or slacks and knit tops, but today, she'd donned a dusky blue dress with a navy stripe that accentuated the gray of her eyes—a violet gray like heather.

"What are you going to have?" he asked. "I'm ordering bacon with the mile-high stack of pancakes."

She sent him a wry grin. "That's because you're a mile high. I'm a shrimp, but that's not on the menu." She tucked her hair behind her ear and refocused on the menu. "I think I'll have a two-egg omelet with an English muffin."

"You'll waste away."

"Don't be silly." She slid the menu onto the table and sipped the coffee, her gaze searching his as if she had questions to ask.

"What's on your mind?" he asked.

"Just wondering." Her fingers circled the cup.

"Wondering what?"

"About you. What made you decide to be a Christian youth worker, for example?"

"That's a funny story," he said, rubbing the back of his neck. "I'd planned to be a coach and phys ed teacher. I loved gym class in high school." His mind flew back to his folks' frustration with his low marks in math but straight As in phys ed.

"You must have done well in other subjects since you made it through college."

"I wasn't too bad," he said, "but I worked hard for some grades. . .like math."

"Math wasn't my favorite either." She leaned forward on her elbows and grinned. "You still haven't answered me. Why did you become a youth director?"

"When I headed for college, my parents weren't thrilled with my phys ed choice, but I was determined—do or die. I do have an occasional flaw."

"Really. I can add that to your unwillingness to carry the EpiPen."

"It's the same problem. I'm stubborn at times."

Her face brightened. "Glad to hear I'm not the only sinner."

"Not by a long shot," he said, pushing away the list of his flaws. God knew his flaws, but why admit them to Lana until they were evident? The thought made him smile.

"You're also evasive. Tell me why you became a youth minister."

She'd caught him again, and he grinned. "Like I said, I was determined to go into coaching. You know, be a phys ed teacher. But when it was time to go through registration, I stood in line clutching those forms, and a strange sensation came over me. Something inside me gnawed and pushed until my fingers gripped the pen and filled in my classes without my consent."

"Huh?" She tilted her head, her face was charged with bewilderment.

"I felt the same way you look, Lana. Puzzled. Perplexed. All I can say is God's will pushed my pen that day. I changed my major to leadership and specialized in youth ministry."

She gave him a blank stare. "You mean God filled out your college registration?"

"He pushed my pen. . .but the choice hadn't been mine."

"Are you sorry?" A frown wrinkled her freckled forehead.

"Not one bit. Youth ministry is my calling. God had to hit me over the head a little, but I finally came to the realization that working with kids in a church setting was what I was meant to do." Another truth crossed his mind. "And my career strengthened my faith even more than I could imagine."

Her frown had vanished, replaced by interest. "So how did your parents feel about that choice?"

"They loved it. My folks. . ." He halted as the breakfast fare appeared in front of them. He eyed his huge stack of pancakes and slabs of bacon, then focused on Lana's small omelet and muffin.

"Anything else?" the waiter asked.

"You can refill the coffee," Mark said.

The young man nodded and left.

"Would you like me to say the blessing?" Mark asked, taking each of Lana's hands in his.

She nodded, and they bowed their heads while he thanked God for the food and their friendship. He gave her fingers a squeeze before he released them. Then he eyed his pancakes and picked up his fork.

"Thanks," Lana said, a gentle look in her eyes. She tried her omelet and then cornered him again. "So what about your folks? What did they think about your choice?"

Mark chuckled at her inquisitiveness. "You mean I don't even get one bite?"

"Go ahead. I can wait, but I'm interested."

He forked into the pancakes dripping with butter, then after the first bite, added some maple syrup. The next taste left him with a pleasant sweetness clinging to his lips, and his mind drifted to Lana. . .and her lips. *Would her kiss be as sweet?* Surprised at his mind's journey, he refocused on the breakfast and pushed the romantic thoughts from his mind.

When he'd satisfied his hunger, Mark washed the syrup away with hot coffee and returned to Lana's question. "My folks were active Christians, so they were thrilled when I decided to focus on church work." He rubbed his neck and chuckled. "I suppose if I'd been a city road worker, they would have been supportive. They've always been that way."

"Where did you grow up?" Lana asked. "Around here?" A piece of English muffin stood poised in her grasp.

"In Michigan. We lived in Warren while I was in high school. Now my folks live in Sterling Heights. You know where that is?"

She nodded. "I grew up in Fenton. My parents are still there, but after college, Barb and I decided to live on our own. I like my independence."

"I suspected that," he said, giving her a knowing smile.

She nibbled on the muffin, then picked up the napkin and patted her mouth. "So how do you know my neighbor Jim?"

"Whoa. Let's talk about you first," Mark said. "What's fair is fair."

"What's that mean?" She eyed him with suspicion.

"What do you mean, what does that mean?" He shook his head. "You made me tell you my life story. Now let's hear yours." He delved into the pancakes again, looking forward to a break.

"I hate talking about me."

"Too bad," he said through his mouthful of pancakes.

"Just tell me about Jim," she countered. "Then I'll talk about me."

Remembering her persistence, he swallowed his mouthful and gave in. "Jim and I met in college. We were roommates for a couple of years until I got my own apartment."

"He didn't move with you?"

"We realized even though we were friends and had some things in common, we had a few things that clashed." Mark felt the sting of his words. He'd been the one to move out, and when Jim had asked about moving in with him, Mark had suggested it wasn't a good idea. Jim had been hurt by his decision.

"How did you clash?" She took another forkful of omelet.

He knew she'd ask. "He has different beliefs than I do. That's the main thing."

"You mean religious beliefs? I notice he doesn't seem to go to church."

"He doesn't, but that wasn't the reason. He drank too much when we were in college. That really bothered me. He seems to handle it better now, but I didn't want to be around it." If he were baring his soul, he needed to tell her the whole story. He studied her serious face for a moment before continuing. "To be honest, my faith wasn't as strong then. I felt myself tempted to follow along. You know, be part of the group."

She looked at the tabletop and nodded. "It's what kids tend to do, isn't it?" She lifted serious eyes to his. "At least you've admitted your failing."

"I felt guilty. . .like I should have been stronger. I am now." He chuckled. Since he was spilling his faults out on the table, he might as well barrel along. "But I'm still not perfect."

"Aha. Another flaw. Stubborn, determined, and not perfect.

I'm tallying this in self-defense."

He grinned, but saw her face grow serious again. "So what about now? You're staying with Jim."

"I tried talking to him when we were in college. It never worked. Now I just offer a few gentle comments, hoping one day it'll sink in.

"That's what you have to do, I suppose. If you push too hard, a person pushes back."

She'd spoken the truth. He'd teased her a little about her impatience, but pushing wouldn't do any good. He'd seen it in himself. Anyway, he had a long way to go with perfection. He hid his private grin. If change happened, it had to be the sinner's decision with lots of help from the Lord.

"I'm surprised you and Jim are still friends," Lana said, nudging her plate away and resting her cheek on her propped-up fist.

"That's my fault." He released his tethered smile. "I don't like to make enemies or lose friends. He was upset when I moved out, but he got over it. I think he understood in the long run. When I was called to First Church of Holly, I knew he lived in town. I called him, and he offered me a place to stay. He's a nice guy. . .and like I said, I'm a stronger Christian now. . . even with my faults."

A truth struck Mark that he needed to remember. The teens would grow in their faith as they became adults. Working with them, he couldn't push like he wanted to sometimes. He had to be firm but compassionate.

He pulled himself from his thoughts and focused on Lana. "Okay. I answered your questions. Now it's my turn to ask. Tell me why you became a teacher." He'd wondered about that since she'd mentioned not being fond of teenagers.

"My parents' idea." She blinked a couple times before continuing. "They were willing to help me finance college if I picked a sensible career." She shrugged. "Teaching seemed sensible to them."

"But what about your own interests?" He couldn't believe she'd become a teacher for her parents.

"You just told me God signed you up for church work. Why can't my parents sign me up for teaching?" A silly grin settled on her face. "Just teasing," she said. "When I was younger, I thought I wanted to be a nurse. I suppose all kids do. I felt the qualities of a nurse fit my skills."

"For sure," Mark said. "Organization, authority, details. A nurse with the marines. Am I right?" He playfully patted her hand.

"No," she said, giving him a ferocious scowl, "but it doesn't matter. As I said earlier, my math wasn't great either, and my science was even worse. So I got realistic."

"Realistic?"

"My parents are practical people. Dad is a factory worker in Flint. Automobiles. He worked to provide all our needs, and my mom's a homebody. I needed to study something sensible."

Empathy nudged at his emotions, but her analogy made him chuckle. "So you became a teacher and hate it."

"No, not really. I suppose I sound like I hate it. It's just frustrating. Kids have too many problems and not enough guidance. Mothers and fathers both work while teens are left on their own too much. They want everything handed to them. They don't want to figure out anything. At least that's the way it seems."

"And that's why I'm a youth director. Even Christian kids fall into that rut—like I did. They need to find out no matter how busy their parents are, Jesus is walking along with them. God is on their side. If they need help and they can't talk with their parents, turn to the Lord in prayer. . .or maybe, their youth director."

Lana grinned. "My parents would have considered a church youth director practical and sensible too."

"What about Barb?" he asked. "What does she do?"

"She went to business school and works in an office. That's—"

"Very sensible," he said.

She laughed, but the lightness faded, and in its place, her face shifted to a more serious expression. "I know I drive people crazy with my organization and details. I was the oldest, and my parents emphasized being on time and always doing my best. It just stuck, I guess. When I was a kid, I wanted to please them. Now I can't seem to forget that need. I'm still trying to please them, but I'm not making myself happy. I get frustrated at my own flaws and inabilities, and I don't like to deal with disorganized, tardy, abstract people."

"Nothing wrong with being on time and being organized." He slid his arm across the table and rested his palm against her silky arm. "You just have to remember that not everyone has those skills."

"Be patient, you mean?"

He nodded. "Patience is a virtue. . .a fruit of the Spirit. And the Holy Spirit's ready to develop more such qualities in your life if you ask for them."

"You think so?"

"Bible says so."

She grinned. "It does. That's true."

Her expression shifted like food in a blender, and Mark suspected she was delving for a comeback.

"Let's see. Stubborn. Determined. So," she said, giving him a mischievous look, "let's talk more about you."

three

Clipping off a dead branch, Mark heard a voice and looked up.

"What are you doing?" Lana's face appeared through the kitchen window screen.

"Finishing my job. You hired me, didn't you?"

She flagged away his comment. "Then tried to poison you. So you're back for more?"

He laughed, delighting in her humor. "You don't see me eating anything, do you?" He patted his belly. "Besides I have to work off the pancakes from breakfast."

"Sounds like an excuse. You're just determined."

He grinned and tallied a point for her into the air with his index finger. She'd begun to know him too well.

"It's Sunday. I thought we're supposed to rest." Her face vanished from the open window, and in a moment, he heard the garage access door open. She came through the doorway carrying a rake. "If we're worried about breakfast calories, then I need the exercise too."

Mark loved watching her expressive face, the way her head tilted and her nose wrinkled—a nose dappled with freckles, and a natural smile that sent his pulse on a gallop. "Don't you have anything better to do?"

"My lesson plans are finished for the week. We have only three days of classes because final exams start this Thursday. After three test days and two more for grading and cleanup, I'm free." She lifted her shoulders in a deep sigh.

"Then let's get busy." Mark motioned toward the fallen twigs from the shrub. "You can rake those in a pile."

Lana eyed the scattered clippings and headed across the lawn,

36

stretching her arms and dragging the debris into a neat pile.

Mark stood a moment, admiring her energy; her slender arms pulling at the rake and her short stature gave no evidence to her bigger-than-life personality. But not a big heart—from what she said.

He wondered why a lovely young woman like Lana possessed such a negative outlook on teens. The attitude just didn't fit. She wasn't that old herself. Probably three or four years younger than his twenty-nine years. He longed to probe but not until he knew her better. Maybe in time she would tell him what bothered her.

Glancing his way, Lana paused and leaned on the rake. "If you're stopping, so am I." She sent him a wry smile.

He shrugged playfully and turned back to the trimming, but she stayed in his mind. The way her gray eyes squinted in the sunshine. The way the sunlight accentuated the red streaks in her light brown hair falling in wayward straggles over her forehead. The way her small stature seemed elfinlike. . .yet delicate and lovely.

When he turned her way, she'd disappeared, leaving a pile of dead twigs and trimmings in a tidy pile along with the rake. Before he could wonder where she'd gone, she reappeared with two shiny red apples. She strode toward him in her purposeful way and offered him a piece of fruit. He took one from her, and his teeth dug into the crisp, juicy Braeburn. The snap of the skin sounded in his ears, and the sweetness rolled on his tongue while the juice ran down his chin.

Lana laughed and pulled a napkin from her jeans pocket. She handed him one. "Always thinking ahead."

Organization seemed her gift and her bane. Details could be part of her problem. She had no patience for those spur-of-the-moment souls who enjoyed adventures in life rather than mapping out each strategy. Just like he'd always been determined to do things his way.

They ate their apples, talking about nothing important, and when they finished, Lana held out a paper towel. "I'll throw the core away," she said, extending the toweling toward him.

Mark grasped the apple fragments. "Toss it into the shrubs. The birds will eat it, and if not, it'll work as compost. It's great for the soil."

Her expression let him know she didn't like the idea.

"You don't have to," he added.

He could see her mentally struggling with his suggestion. Finally she tucked the towel back into her pocket. "If you don't think the neighbors will accuse me of throwing garbage in my yard. . ."

"I don't think so," he said, tossing the apple core into the tall hedge along the fence.

With much effort, she followed his example, and in his heart, Mark congratulated her for doing something spur of the moment. Something unplanned and natural.

Returning to his pruning, Mark enjoyed the smell of the spring loam, rich from the winter's decay. New growth surrounded him, and he suspected Lana exhibited new growth too.

The word "new" prodded him with another thought. He needed to find an apartment or flat—some place to call home. In the interim, Jim had been gracious to invite him to stay at his place, but he realized his presence limited Jim's way of life—a life that was guided by different values than Mark's. He didn't judge, but he believed God's Word. Mark tried hard to live a life that God would approve.

"Looks good," Lana said, appearing at his side and pulling him from his thoughts.

"It does, if I do say so myself." He grinned at her upturned face.

"So. . .will another dinner minus peanuts cover my indebtedness?" She rolled her eyes and shook her head, faltering.

"I don't think so." Teasing, Mark slid his arm around her

shoulder. "I have plans for you," he said, startled by the excitement that rolled through him with his touch.

"Plans?" Her voice sounded suspicious.

"How about letting me borrow your newspaper? I need to do some apartment hunting. Do you think it's too late?" He checked his watch. Six o'clock.

She eyed hers and shrugged. "Maybe a little late."

"Okay. How's this? I'll check the paper, and you can help since you know the area. We'll make a list, and tomorrow you'll go along with me."

She stood in silence a moment, then nodded. "Okay. I suppose I should be neighborly, but. . .what about dinner?"

"Let's order pizza. Easier and safer. I've never had pizza with peanuts."

Lana grasped his arm, giving it a teasing shake. "Then you've never had my homemade pizza."

Enjoying the earlier sensation, Mark slipped his arm around her shoulder as they headed for the house. Unbidden thoughts slithered into his mind. He needed to know Lana much better before allowing his heart to get tangled with hers. Now all he had to do was convince his heart to pay attention to his warning.

❧

Lana did a full turn, scrutinizing the kitchen. Ugly cabinets, little counter space, old appliances. Mark couldn't live in a place like this. She eyed the newspaper ad they'd looked at the evening before. The whole thing seemed full of untruths. "Look, it says right here," she said, pointing to the paper, " 'cozy apartment.' "

Mark clasped the back of her neck, giving it a gentle squeeze. "Some people's cozy is another person's misery."

"But you're smiling," she said, amazed at his optimism. "They didn't tell the truth." She tapped her finger against the want-ad listing. "Right here in the paper."

"They exaggerated," he said. "And remember. . .never believe everything you read in the news."

His good humor nudged at her frustration, shifting it an inch. "Let's try the next place."

"Okay, but don't get your head in a whirl with any preconceived notions." He steered her through the doorway and down the stairs. At the apartment supervisor's door, Mark dropped off the key, then headed to the car.

"The ads are always so disappointing and discouraging," Lana said. "Before we bought the house, Barb and I looked for a rental to share. We were so frustrated."

"You have to take a lot of the details with the proverbial grain of salt," Mark said.

A grain of salt. Mark seemed to do that. He looked at life with an open mind, willing to take whatever came his way with that proverbial grain of salt he'd mentioned, like the day Barb brought him home to clean the yard. He'd done it with a smile.

"Here's an idea," he said, jolting her from her thoughts. He took one hand from the steering wheel and motioned toward the newspaper on the seat beside her. "Read me the next ad. We can speculate what the reality might be."

His good nature dragged a grin to her face. She picked up the paper and scanned the listing until she found the ad. "Here goes. Five-room apartment." She stopped. "Let's see. We can expect two rooms. Right?"

He shook his head. "Four rooms and bath—living room, kitchen, bedroom, and. . .foyer."

She gave him a presumptuous look. "An entry's not a room."

"But it is in newspaper ads."

She poked his arm. "You're being silly." Focusing on the paper, she ran her finger along the column to find the ad. "Good location, it says here. What about that?'"

"It doesn't say good for what, does it?"

Mark was surprised by her laughter.

"What about this?" she asked. "Spotless." She held up her palm, halting him. "Don't tell me." She rested her finger beside her mouth. "Painted only five years ago and adequately clean."

"You got it," he said, pleased that she'd jumped in with the silly definitions. "Now you won't be disappointed." He glanced her way and prayed she could handle whatever they found.

When he saw Oak Street, he turned left and checked addresses. In the second block, he felt pleasantly surprised. Two neat rows of single-story apartments stood face-to-face, divided by a long driveway that led to a carport beside each unit. The grounds were neat, and a small tree shaded each front yard. But behind the buildings, Mark could see taller trees—oaks and elms towering over the rooftops. So far, so good.

He eyed Lana, and her expression looked positive. "A carport's nice. Keeps the snow off."

"And I like the trees," he said, motioning to the tall branches evident behind the buildings. "Wait here, and I'll get the key."

He darted to the first apartment, and when he returned, a gentleman followed along.

"Hello there," the man said, giving Lana a nod. "I'll unlock the door for you so you can take a peek." He gestured toward the apartment on the end of the complex.

Lana liked the wide windows at the front and the building's neat appearance.

"Now you take your time," the man said as he turned the key and opened the door. "You two look like a nice, friendly couple. I hope you like the place."

"We. . .I'm. . ." Lana's voice trailed off, and she eyed Mark, waiting for him to respond. Heat rose to her cheeks.

Mark sent her a toying grin and nodded at the man. "Thanks. We'll let you know when we're finished."

The gentleman nodded his head and turned back toward his apartment while Lana gaped at Mark, confused.

"What's the sense of disappointing him?" Mark asked. "He thought we were a nice, friendly couple."

His smile sent Lana's heart reeling. He was only teasing her. That seemed Mark's way. His crazy sense of humor.

She followed his gesture and stepped into a small foyer with a coat closet. "First room," Lana said with a laugh.

"We'll have to see," Mark said good-naturedly. He walked through the large living room and down a hallway to a fair-sized bedroom and bath, noticing with pleasure the place did look spotless.

Lana followed behind him, but her wary gaze held a new hint of optimism. "The carpet looks like its been cleaned recently," she said.

Mark agreed. The medium gray carpet seemed fairly new. Inside the bedroom, he opened a large double-door closet. "See. Not bad and an extra big closet."

"Maybe it's large because that's the fifth room," she said, then sent him a teasing smile.

They retraced their steps and entered a roomy kitchen with plenty of cabinets. The appliances looked well kept, and the room had ample table space. But the surprise hit him at another doorway. "Look." He motioned to Lana. "A sun room, and it's heated so it's year-round."

Her eyes widened. "You mean this really is a fifth room."

"Looks like it," he said, thrilled at what they'd found. He gazed out the wide windows at the tree-filled setting. "What a great place to enjoy the outdoors even in winter and still be warm."

"The owners outdid themselves on this place," Lana admitted. "This is really a nice rental."

"You admit you were wrong about newspaper ads?"

"Wrong about one ad."

"Where there's one, there's hope. Just keep that in mind," he said, beckoning her through the front door. "This is it as far as I'm concerned."

"It's great, Mark. Why not give the man your deposit?"

She caressed his shoulder, and a sweet feeling ran down his arm. He loved to see her smile and rejoice with him. Could this be God's direction? He prayed it was.

❧

Lana stood in her classroom doorway and spied Stacy Leonard talking with a friend. Her anger seemed evident, and Lana held back, not wanting to get involved. But Stacy lifted her gaze and saw Lana watching her. The teenager slammed her locker and headed her way.

"What's wrong, Stacy?" Lana asked. The girl looked as if she'd planned to scoot past, but Lana felt compelled to stop her.

"Nothing." She rolled her eyes and looked at the ceiling.

"For nothing wrong, you seem mighty upset." Lana held her ground and kept the girl in direct focus.

"It's nothing that concerns you. You wouldn't understand anyway," Stacy said.

"Why don't you try me?"

"I'm just tired of having my plans goofed up. I had everything organized, then my friend tossed in her own plans and. . . I'm tired of it." Stacy's head lowered, and Lana suspected she had tears in her eyes.

"I'm sorry your friend didn't take your plans seriously. Sometimes two people's ideas clash, and if we want to remain friends, we have to compromise. I'm sure you've heard that before." Lana rolled her eyes and grinned.

A faint smile crept to Stacy's face. "We were supposed to spend the night together at my house, but now she wants to go to the movies first, and unless I lie to my parents about what we're doing, they won't let me go."

"Sounds like you don't want to tell your parents a fib."

Lana prayed she was correct.

Stacy shook her head. "If I do, they'll find out anyway. They always do."

"Truth is easier, isn't it?"

The girl nodded. "But now she'll go off with other friends and party while I sit home alone."

"Can you talk with her? Maybe you can suggest something different that your parents will approve. Roller skating. . .or hanging out at a mall." Lana grasped at ideas, hoping she might hit on something that would help.

"The mall? She might like that idea."

Lana could almost hear the girl's mind working through ideas. "You see. Compromise can work. You just have to remove the emotion and think with reason."

Stacy laughed. "If you ask my parents, they don't think I'm very reasonable."

"Parents worry a lot about their kids."

Stacy's face had brightened, and she took a step backward. "Thanks, Miss West. I'll call Julie and see if she'd like to go the mall instead."

"Good for you," Lana said, sending the girl a wave as she sped away.

Lana turned into her classroom. Only the weekend and then three more days before school closed. Her own plans filtered through her mind. This summer she'd decided to redecorate her bedroom. She had some great stenciling ideas for refurbishing her old dresser and headboard. When she finished that job, Lana had plans to tackle the dining room—paint and add a border where a chair molding would be. Her list had grown, and no one could stop her.

She faltered, recognizing Stacy's complaint as her own. She hated people to botch up her plans, and although she'd given Stacy good advice, compromise wasn't Lana's favorite way to solve a problem. Not at all.

✍

Mark left his car in the street and headed into Jim's place. He had a little packing to do, and tonight, he had bowling with the teens. Not his favorite activity, but it was his job. Tomorrow, he looked forward to getting into his own apartment. As he rounded his sedan, Lana came down the driveway toward the mailbox. He gave her a wave, and she returned his greeting.

"Tomorrow's the big day," he said. "My furniture comes out of storage."

"You're moving tomorrow?" Her face shifted through a medley of emotions and settled on an amiable smile.

He strode toward her. "I could use a woman's touch getting settled. . .and I know you don't work on Saturdays."

She fingered her top button and thought for a moment. "Living next door, I'm at your mercy." Her grin looked more natural than the earlier smile. "I'm not good at carrying. I'm too short. . .and weak."

"How about small boxes? You can handle those."

She nodded.

"And unpacking. You can do that if I open the box."

"Got me," she said, giving him a poke. "You sound like you think I'm trying to wheedle out of helping you."

"Aren't you the lady who said you hated doing things for other people?" He sent her a knowing gaze.

Amused, she winced playfully. "Me and my big mouth. I need to learn to keep it shut." She pulled the mail out of the box and shut the lid.

"Too late. I already know that little tidbit of information." He patted her shoulder. "So I can count on you?"

"Why not? My exams are all ready. No papers to grade. The clock is ticking down, and a smile is rising." She sent him a toothy grin.

"Now that you shared that piece of news, I have another idea."

She did a quick two-step backward. "Sorry, I can't hear you." Her feet carried her farther away.

He beckoned her toward him, and she grudgingly acquiesced.

"What?" she asked, tilting her head with a pitiful frown.

"It's this way." He took his finger and lifted the corners of her mouth, forcing them into a grin. "I have to do something tonight I'm not crazy about. . .and I thought maybe you'd like to join me."

Her forced grin grew into a real smile. "Now there's an offer that's hard to pass up." She glanced at her mail, then tapped it against her cheek. "So what not-crazy-about activity are you asking me to participate in? Bungee jumping off a bridge? Sky diving from a jet?"

"Sounds like you aren't crazy about heights."

"That and snakes. Don't ask me to do anything that involves either of those things."

She looked squeamish just mentioning snakes, and her expression tickled him. "No snakes. No heights. You're safe."

"Safe? I doubt that. What did you have in mind?"

"Bowling." He watched her face turn from fear of snakes to disgust. "Apparently you're not fond of that activity either."

"I hate it. What fun is it to roll a fat, heavy ball down a narrow lane and knock down a few wooden sticks?" She rolled her eyes and shook her head.

"Teenagers. They love it. It's not bowling. It's the camaraderie. . .and that's what I need. A friend and, better yet, a friend who knows some of the kids. You'd be so helpful."

"I can't bowl."

"Okay, you can keep score." He gave her his most optimistic look.

He could see her mind conjuring up something important she had to do.

"Your hair looks fine," he said. "You don't need a shampoo." He clasped her free hand, and its smallness sent a sensation skidding through his chest. He gazed at her fingernails. "Manicure looks good." He worked to keep his voice steady. "No excuses."

She covered her face with the handful of mail and laughed. "Wow! You're hard to discourage."

"Come along—please. You'll give me adult conversation, and all you have to do is keep score. I'll show you how." He recreated the pleading look from his childhood that worked miracles on his mother and sent it Lana's way.

She shook her head. "Scorekeeper, and that's it."

"It's a deal," he said.

four

"Come on, Miss West," Gary said. "You can't just keep score. Everyone bowls."

Lana looked at the lanes of bowlers and sent a pleading look to Mark. "You promised."

He shrugged. "No, I only said it's a deal."

She gripped the black marker and clutched the chair with her free fingers. She wasn't planning to budge. Bowling came right in there next to having her tooth filled without benefit of Novocain.

"Come on, Miss West." Three other teens joined Gary, their pleading voices sailing across the surrounding lanes.

Embarrassed at the attention, Lana dropped the marker. "Fine. I have to rent shoes and find a ball." She strode away, trying to keep a cooperative look on her face, but fearing that she had failed.

With red, white, and blue rented shoes announcing her size five on the back and a ball that seemed far too heavy to lift, she returned to the group and plopped onto the bench. The teens had already begun to bowl, and she watched the pins teetering, then dropping to the floor while cheers rose and shouts of spare or strike reverberated to the high ceiling.

She looked at the alley next to hers where Mark stood poised, the ball clasped in his gripping fingers and resting on his other hand. He crouched down and took four quick steps, swinging the ball back, then bringing it forward and releasing it smoothly onto the highly polished surface of the lane. The black ball sped toward the pins, hooking left just before it slammed into them and vanished into the darkness. Lana watched the white pins tumble to the ground except for one that wobbled and then remained upright.

"You'll get this one," a voice urged. "A spare's good, Mark."

Surprised that the boy had called his youth director "Mark," Lana watched the kids cheer when moments later the single pin went flying. She frowned in thought. Mark—and she was Miss West. But wasn't that how it should be? Respect and authority?

"You're up, Miss West," Susan said.

Lana looked down at her clown shoes and rose, grasping the ball. She stuck her fingers into the three holes, hoping she'd done it correctly, and carried the object as if it were a ball and chain.

She remembered what Mark had done and paused in front of the black line, but before she could move, Mark stepped beside her.

"Back up a little, or you'll step over the line," he said, guiding her by the shoulders.

"I know," she said, taking a couple of steps back. She should have told Mark. Not only couldn't she bowl well, she'd never bowled in her life. Later she would tell him, but not in front of the kids.

"Haven't you ever bowled?" Mark asked, eyeing her.

With his question, he'd saved her the trouble of a confession. She shook her head and whispered, "No. I told you I hate the game."

"Do you want some pointers?" he whispered back.

"No." She sent him a determined look. She didn't want to stand there like a novice while all the teens watched her get a bowling lesson.

"Okay," he said, "just step forward, swing your arm back, and as you swing forward release the ball."

"I know." Telling him she didn't want instructions had been as effective as watering the lawn during a rainstorm.

She grasped her fortitude—along with the ball—took aim, stepped forward, swung back, and released the ball. A thud rang out along with the titters of surrounding bowlers as the ball shot behind her and settled beneath the bench.

"The lane's in front of you, Miss West," Jason called.

She swung around, catching the frown that surged to her face and replaced it with a look she hoped was good-natured.

Jason jumped up and returned the ball. She turned her back, aiming again, but this time clung to the ball with every muscle in her thumb and two fingers. She pranced toward the black line, cautiously swung her arm back, then brought it forward before she released the ball. This time her heart lifted as the blue-and-white beauty spiraled down the lane. But her up-lifted heart sank as the ball took a wide curve and dropped into the gutter.

"Gutter ball," Susan yelled.

She refused to turn around as she waited for the oppressive orb to return. She grasped it again, this time more determined.

"Keep your arm straight and follow through," Mark whispered from the adjacent alley.

She arched an eyebrow, got set, took her steps, swung, and released. The ball went forward. It curved toward the gutter, but this time, it curved back and clipped five pins. Relieved, she spun away and marched back to her seat. How had she gotten herself into this mess?

As her next turn neared, she eyed the score sheet and realized she faced eighteen more opportunities to make a fool of herself—assuming she didn't get any strikes. When she rose again, she uttered a silent prayer. She knew God had more important things to do than worry about her hitting those pins, but she felt utterly mortified, and she hoped the Lord understood. Opening her eyes, she let the ball go, and to her surprise, it rolled down the center of the lane, sending pins flying.

A cheer went up, and when the fallen pins had been cleared

away, only two pins remained standing. The ball returned and she grasped it, feeling more confident. She realized it just took a little time to get the hang of bowling. She focused on the spots, and when she released the ball, her ring finger caught inside the grip holes. The ball flew through the air and thudded about halfway down the alley. While she nursed her throbbing digit, the ball knocked the pins into the air for a spare.

Applause and cheers rose behind her, but when she turned around, the sound died.

"What happened?" Mark asked, pulling away and gaping at her swelling finger.

"I don't know. It seemed to stick in the hole."

While a few teens gawked, Mark studied it a moment. "Looks like a sprain. I'll get some ice from the bar." He rested his hand on her shoulder. "Looks like you'll be sitting out the rest of the frames."

Gratitude tangled with her pain. "Seriously?"

He nodded.

"What a shame. I was just getting the hang of it." She sank to the chair in front of the score sheet and clutched her throbbing finger while she hid her grateful grin.

🐾

Standing in Lana's driveway the next morning, Mark studied her purposeful expression. "Are you sure?"

"Yes. You drive your car, and I'll follow you with the boxes in mine." She lifted the trunk lid and eyed it. "What doesn't fit in the trunk will go into the back seat."

"I can probably cram a couple more things into my trunk," he said again, sure she couldn't get everything into her small-sized vehicle.

"Remember, I'm Miss Organization. Trust me." She clutched her chest, and her splinted finger jarred his memory. Her eyes shifted from him to her bandage and back. "And if you hadn't manipulated me into going bowling, I wouldn't have a sprained finger. Now I'm working with a handicap."

He bit his tongue, wanting to tease her and say her biggest handicap was her lack of patience and stubborn resolve, but she'd hit upon the truth. Another of his flaws. He did try to direct people and situations. "I'm sorry about your finger. I didn't realize the kids would goad you into bowling."

"Neither did I, or I wouldn't have gone." She turned back to the trunk and shifted a couple more boxes.

He'd never known anyone so set on doing something her own way, but he knew pushing her wouldn't work. He thanked the Lord that she hadn't been the one chosen to lead the children of Israel into the Promised Land. They'd still be wandering, lost somewhere in the Himalayas. He could easily imagine Lana bypassing the Red Sea and trying to part the Indian Ocean instead.

"Okay," he reluctantly agreed, "but let's get going. Jim's already on his way with the moving van, and I have the apartment key." He stood back, watching her shuffle and reorganize until she had each item in a specific spot only a mind like Lana's could arrange.

"What else?" she asked, challenging him.

"Clothes. Things from my closet and a bag of shoes. Things like that, but I'll come back for those." She seemed like an immovable mountain, and Mark could tell she wouldn't budge on the issue.

"They'll fit in here. Why come back?" Her petite frame seemed to grow in size.

Giving up, he shrugged and marched inside with Lana behind him. Avoiding her sprained finger, he loaded her arms with bags of shoes, his travel kit with his EpiPens, and a small box of personal items. Then he gathered up his shirts, suits, and trousers—all the things he hadn't packed in his luggage.

They marched to her car, where she slid a couple items onto the roof while she packed the smaller boxes onto the backseat floor. After she'd arranged most of his clothes on the back seat, she took the final pieces from his arms.

"You go ahead, and I'll be there in a minute. I know Jim's waiting. I only have these last things to pack."

He stood empty-armed, figuring he'd be safe leaving and certain he'd arrive at least a half hour before she would. "Okay. I'll meet you there."

She gave him a wave, and he headed down the driveway. Without looking back, he climbed into his car and pulled away from the curb. What a woman. Why did he feel so attracted to her? A stubborn, impatient woman didn't seem to fit the description of the ideal partner for a youth director. But when he thought of Lana, instead of picturing that determined look, he remembered her casual grace and warm, teasing smile. She made him laugh. Maybe God had given him a challenge so he might learn humility and guidance. . .or maybe Lana would learn something from him. Patience and optimism, perhaps.

He grinned, wondering if God had the patience for either one of them.

When Mark pulled in front of his apartment, Jim was waiting, leaning against the back of the moving van.

"I thought you got lost," Jim said, pulling open the double door of the truck. "Let's unload the furniture first. If I can get this truck back early, it'll save you a few bucks. Maybe enough for a six-pack of beer."

Mark tried to smile. "No six-pack for me, Jim. I work with kids, remember? I need to be a good example." He whacked Jim's paunchy belly with the back of his fist. "Plus I don't want to lose my youthful physique. Before you know it, you won't be able to bend over and tie your shoes."

Jim only grinned, but Mark hoped his words sent a cautious warning into his friend's mind.

Mark joined Jim at the truck, and together they carried in the mattress and box spring, then the rest of the bedroom furniture and the sofa, one piece at a time. While they toted in the boxes, Lana pulled into the driveway.

"We're taking in this load first," he said. Knowing she'd be antsy waiting, he added, "But if you can dodge around us, you can hang the clothes in my closet if you want."

She nodded and opened the back door of the car.

He moved ahead into the house and grinned, watching Lana stay out of their way without a squeak until the truck was emptied.

When Jim left with the trailer, Mark and Lana finished unpacking her car, and after everything was inside, he stood in the living room and surveyed the situation. "Here's what we can do. A woman's comfort zone is the kitchen." Then, thinking of their near mishaps, he laughed. "Let me rephrase that. With your unique skills, I'll let you set up the kitchen. . . and don't worry. I even have a step stool."

"All the modern conveniences," Lana said. "And what will you do? Watch the ball game?" She tilted her head toward the television.

"I'll unpack my clothes and handle the bedroom," he said.

"Sounds like a deal." She headed into the kitchen.

In the bedroom, Mark arranged his clothes in the dresser drawers and listened to the sounds coming from the kitchen. The ting and clang of dishes and pans assured him that Lana was at work. He'd been smart giving her the kitchen task. That's where her skills could shine.

Mark looked around the room for the bag of dress shoes he remembered putting in Lana's car. . .and his travel kit. Besides the EpiPens, he'd tossed his checkbook inside. He suspected they'd never made it to the bedroom and ambled down the hall to look for them. In the living room, boxes still sat unopened, but he saw no sign of the bags he wanted. Concerned, he headed for the kitchen.

"How are you doing?" Mark asked, scanning Lana's progress

from the kitchen doorway.

"Good," she said. "You don't have as much junk as I do."

He laughed "I avoid the kitchen as much as possible." *Maybe so should she.* He chuckled at his thought.

"What's funny?" She pulled open a cabinet door, and he regarded the inside—the contents were arranged in a much more organized and logical fashion than he would have managed. "Just thinking about you in a kitchen."

"Quiet," she said, hurling a dishtowel across the room.

He caught the towel and carried it back to her. "Have you seen the bag with my dress shoes and my travel kit?"

She turned, a thoughtful look on her face. "Not that I remember."

"Could they still be in the car?" He wandered around the room, nosing into the boxes and searching beneath the table and chairs—anywhere in hopes he'd find them.

"No, it's empty. I'm positive," she said, facing him and leaning against the counter. "The last time I saw the travel kit was when I. . ." Her face paled.

"When you what?" Her look sent his stomach on a spiraling journey. "What?" he repeated.

"When I set them on top of the car." She jammed her hair behind her ear and looked as if she might cry.

Their eyes met, and he studied her anxious face.

"I'd planned to put them on the passenger seat after I finished in the back, but I don't remember putting them there."

Mark rubbed the back of his neck. His dress shoes, his allergy medication, razor, and all his other toiletries. "Are you sure?"

She bit her lip and nodded. "I'm so sorry."

"It was an accident," he said, but he couldn't help but mentally tally the cost of replacing everything, and he could, but what about the checkbook? *God will provide,* he said to himself, not wanting to upset Lana.

"I know, but I seem to be a klutz lately," she said. "What happened to those detail skills you razz me about?"

Though troubled, he aimed to appear lighthearted. "They took a vacation before you did." While he spoke, a hopeful thought settled in his mind. "You know, the things may have fallen off in the driveway. I'll take a ride over and see. You stay here and pray."

"Let's call Barb. Maybe she's already found them. If she did, she wouldn't call here. She doesn't know your telephone number."

"Good idea, but let's pray anyway," he said, seeing concern grow on her face. He tried to cover his own distress. He could replace everything. . .but his checkbook worried him.

She lifted the phone, punched in the numbers, and waited. In silence, she hung up and turned to him. "She's not there. The answering machine kicked in."

"I'd better go over to your place, then, and see."

"That's what I figured. No sense in leaving a message for Barb." She tugged on her top button, gloom covering her face. "I'm so sorry, Mark. It's just another example of my imperfections. I had to do it my way. . .and alone. If I hadn't chased you off, you would have seen the things on the car roof."

He could have given her a lecture, but it wasn't the time. Anyway, it would have done little good. Lana had to learn control and patience for herself. . .and that could only be with God's help. At least she hadn't dashed out to her car so she could solve the problem herself.

Unforeseen, she faced him, then moved toward the doorway. "On second thought, let me go home and look. I'm the one who caused the problem."

Mark's last thought slithered to the floor. "No, I'll do it, Lana. You take care of the kitchen."

She followed him to the door but didn't argue, and he was grateful.

The trip was only a matter of blocks, and as he drove, Mark kept his peripheral vision glued to the road, looking for tell-tale signs of his belongings. Seeing nothing, his hope lifted, but when he pulled up to the driveway and stopped short of the spot where Lana's car had been, he saw nothing.

He climbed from the car and walked along the driveway. In a crevice between the driveway and lawn, something caught his eye. An EpiPen. If that had fallen there, where was everything else?

He moved in a full circle, wondering if a neighbor had picked it up for safekeeping or worse a child. If his careless-ness by not closing his kit had caused a child injury, he'd never forgive himself.

The side door flew open, and Mark jerked.

"Mark." Barb stood in the doorway. "Are you missing some of your things?"

With his heart in his throat, he could only nod.

"The stuff's inside. Come on in."

She pushed the screen open, and he took a calming breath before going inside.

"I didn't know you were here," he said, catching his breath. "Lana called, but she got the answering machine."

"I just got in. I'm thankful no one found it." She gestured to the duffel bag and travel kit sitting on the kitchen table. "Can you picture the little kids in the neighborhood playing grown-up in your shoes?"

He unzipped his shaving kit and pulled out the checkbook. "Or writing checks." He gave her a grateful grin.

"Whew! I didn't know that was there. I assumed the stuff was yours. Lana mentioned you were moving today." She pulled out a kitchen chair. "Have a seat. I'll get you a drink."

With his mouth as dry as Death Valley, he accepted the offer. "Let me call Lana first, if you don't mind. I know she's worried."

"Sure thing," she said, pointing toward the telephone.

When he'd heard Lana's relieved exclamation, Mark gave her a quick explanation and hung up. Sliding into the chair, he took a long, cool drink of the iced tea.

"How did your bags get in our driveway?" Barb asked as she joined him at the table.

"Guess," he said, then told her the tale.

"She's a character, isn't she?" Barb shook her head. "I love my sister with all my heart, but she's like a marine sergeant sometimes."

With his mouth full of tea, Mark sputtered. He covered the front of his mouth with his hand in a futile effort to keep from showering the table.

Barb grabbed a paper napkin and slid it across to him. He mopped up the drizzle and shook his head. "I called her something like that a week or so ago."

"How did she take it?" Her smile told him she was joking.

"I think she'd heard it before," he said, remembering when he'd teased her during their after-church breakfast.

"From me." Barb took a swallow of tea and leaned against the chair back. "There, but for the grace of God, go I." She gave him a wry smile. "You know that saying."

Mark nodded. "I'm afraid I admitted my flaws to her—and she won't let me forget them either.

"If we didn't have flaws, we'd be angels or something." She grinned. "Poor Lana got the worst of it since she was the oldest. We have wonderful parents, but our father has always been the kind of man who lets you know what he never had and what you have. Know what I mean?"

Mark nodded again, although not totally sure he understood.

"Dad never had a bicycle, and he spent his life making sure we had a bike. But we always knew to be grateful for it. We spent a lot of our childhood trying to make Dad happy and being the best kids we could be. . .to the point that now I try to save the world while Lana tries to save herself." She lifted the glass and took another drink. "We're a little goofy, I suppose."

"Not goofy. Just unique. But I understand a little better why Lana is who she is."

"She doesn't talk much about herself," Barb said. "Just let her be in charge, and she's happy. It'll get done fast but in her own way."

Mark had seen that demonstrated, but he had to admit that often Lana's way was a good way. He drained the glass and rose. "I'd better get back. Your sister's organizing my kitchen."

"Then you've got it made. She'll put everything on the shelf in alphabetical order. You won't have to guess where to find a thing."

Mark chuckled and gathered his belongings. Thanking Barb for the tea, he headed for his car. So many things made sense now. Lana had good parents, but her well-meaning father expected appreciation. And how does a kid show gratitude? By behaving and being as perfect as possible.

But Barb's words awakened another thought. He also had a problem with trying to direct the world. His father had tried to guide him when he was younger, and he'd fought back. Now he found himself acting like his father—trying to save the world with his will.

Mark closed his eyes as his words drifted up to heaven. *Father, help Lana and me both learn that we cannot save ourselves or anyone. It's only through Your precious gift that we're saved—through Your Son, Jesus. Help us to live that, Lord. . .and soon.*

When he opened his eyes, he turned the key in the ignition and grinned. He'd just given God a real challenge.

five

On Wednesday, the last day before vacation, Lana slid a graded exam onto the corrected pile and grabbed another. She didn't have to use the answer key anymore. After thirty exams, she knew the answers by heart. Catching a movement out of the corner of her eye, she looked toward the doorway.

"Come in, Don. Have a seat."

Don Fabrizio stepped through the doorway and ambled across the floor. He eased his long legs beneath a front desk and wove his fingers together.

She rose from her desk and stood in front of him. "I'm sorry I had to throw you out of the exam Monday, Don, but you know you were cheating. I saw you. I don't understand why you did that."

He shrugged and stared down at his fingers clutched together on the desk. "So what do you want?"

"I want to know why you cheated. You're not a bad student. In fact, your grades are pretty good. So what's wrong?"

"I didn't study. I couldn't remember all that stuff."

"Why didn't you study?" Lana asked, watching his nervous behavior.

He responded with another shrug, his focus never leaving the desktop.

"I shouldn't give you another chance, but I'm willing if you are," she said, amazed at her decision.

With her offer, his head lifted, and his gaze sought hers. "What do you mean?"

"Another chance," she repeated. "I'll give you a different exam. I always prepare more than one version since I have three classes that are the same."

"You mean. . .you'll let me. . ." He paused as if disbelieving.

"Yes," she said. "You might not do well, but you know I'll have to mark your final grade down horribly if you don't take it at all."

"I know," he said, his voice distant and sad. "And I'd never hear the end of it."

Alerted by his words, Lana searched the boy's face for a hint of his trouble. If he could only talk and tell her what was wrong, he might have some relief from his problem. Her thought stopped her cold. Once again, she saw her own behavior in the teen. How many times had she avoided telling others the things that troubled her. She knew it would seem so unimportant to anyone else, and the telling made her feel vulnerable. Better to keep her thoughts inside and deal with them privately.

"I don't like to talk about my problems either," Lana confessed.

Again, Don lifted his face to hers, his gaze seeming to beg to believe she understood.

"Look, Don," she said, sliding into the desk beside him. "Here's the deal. You tell me why you didn't study, and I'll give you another exam. Fair?"

His face drained of color, and she sensed he was about to rise from the chair and leave. She watched his arms brace against the desk and his foot shift to stand.

Instead, he caved back against the desk and shook his head. "It's too difficult to talk about my family. And nothing I say will change anything."

Lana heard her own thoughts coming from the boy, and sadness rolled through her. She'd spent a lot of time letting her past—a good past really—get in the way of a full life. At least she'd maintained a sense of humor. Quick wit. That's one thing she loved about Mark. The phrase sizzled through her. *Loved about Mark.* Had she really meant what she said?

She drew her attention back to Don, his face strained by

unhappiness. "No, you can't change your family, but you can change yourself and how you react to the family. That's all I can offer you."

"What do you mean change myself?" He released a bitter sigh. "It's my dad who drinks and acts crazy when he gets home at one in the morning. He wakes everyone up, kicking the furniture or else yelling so loud even God couldn't sleep."

God? Was Don a believer? She struggled to decide where to go with the discussion. She couldn't just tell him to give the problem over to God. She knew how she'd struggled with that and failed. He needed more, but he needed the Lord too.

"The other night," Don continued, "he came in early. . .but stupid drunk as usual. I was trying to study, and he kept poking at me and grabbing my study notes. If anyone had seen him besides my family, I'd have died. He acted like a nutcase. I wanted to scream at him or blast him one, but he's my dad."

Don lifted his face to Lana, and she saw the teen's longing to love his father unconditionally. Hope filled his face, and it tugged at Lana's heartstrings.

"I'm sure that was terrible," was all she could find to say. She'd never known a life like that.

"The worst thing was. . .he t–tore up my study notes." He choked on the words.

"Tore them? Why?" She struggled to keep her face from showing emotion.

"For fun."

His answer settled in her stomach like a mountain. How could she respond to this hurting young man? "You had a bad time, Don. Do you have friends you can study with next time? Go to their house. . .or even the library?"

"I don't have many friends. Who wants to invite someone over to see their dad acting like that? And I can't hang out at the guys' homes without having them over. I just gave up."

She grasped at his earlier reference. "Do you believe in

God?" Her silent prayer soared to heaven, asking for wisdom.

He nodded. "My mom taught us about the Bible. She used to read us stories about Jesus, but we don't go to church much."

"I have a friend who. . .he's the youth director of First Church of Holly. Do you know where that is?"

He nodded. "It's not too far from my house."

She felt God's prodding. "Here's an idea. First Church has a nice youth group. They go bowling and. . .all kinds of things." Her mind went blank, and she tried to imagine what else they did. "They don't meet at private houses usually because they have the church. Some of the kids who are members there you might know from Holly High. Why not come to church some Sunday and check it out? You can see what the youth group is doing."

He listened to her without making his escape, and she prayed he'd accept her invitation.

He shrugged. "I don't know. I hate going places alone."

"Well, bring along a friend. And remember that you're not really alone, Don." Mark's words soared into her mind. "Jesus is always walking along with you, and God is on your side." She filled with relief, thanking God for Mark's words. "And you know me too. I realize I'm old, but I'm still your 'old' friend."

He laughed for the first time. "Thanks, Miss West. I'll think about it."

She gathered her wits and returned to the reason he'd come. "Okay, you kept your part of the deal. So if you want to take a look at this exam, maybe you'll do better than you think."

He nodded and settled into the seat, leaning forward to pull the stub of a pencil from his back pocket.

Lana selected a blank exam from her packet and slid it in front of him. "Take your time. There's nothing tricky. The test is asking you to think more than repeat dates and events. Just use your common sense. . .and a little bit of what you learned in class."

He smiled again and bent his head over the test.

Lana returned to correcting papers and averaging grades. She'd already cleaned her room, stripped the bulletin boards, and stored away her teaching materials. At three o'clock she would be a free woman. . .as long as her grade books and sheets were turned in. She could pick up her paycheck and go home.

Home. She had the whole summer to do the projects she'd thought about. Shame filled her. All she had on her mind to worry about had been summer projects. Don had too many worries for a teenager. She lifted her head and eyed him. She thought she'd led a difficult life. She'd lived in bliss compared to this young man.

Again Mark came to mind. Now that he'd moved, she wondered how often she would see him. Maybe it had worked out for the best. His life seemed so devoted compared to hers— giving his time and his talents to make others happy.

She glanced at her wristwatch. Nearly three. Anxious to turn in her grades and leave, she glanced at Don. To her pleasant surprise, he shuffled his test papers in order and rose. "Thanks, Miss West. I know I didn't get an A, but I don't think I failed it either."

"That's great, Don. Have a nice summer, and remember what I said. If you have a chance, drop by the church. I'm sure you won't be sorry."

He nodded, slid the exam onto her desk, and went through the door. She stared at the vacated space for a moment, praying that God would move the boy to come to the church. With a sigh, she pulled his paper in front of her and began to correct his exam.

When she finished, she tallied his grade and averaged the results. Don had been correct. He hadn't failed, and he'd gotten a C minus. Not great but better than a zero. She piled her grade book, report sheets, and exams into a neat pile to turn into the office.

As she rose, a familiar figure appeared at her doorway.

"What are you doing here?" she asked, surprised to see Mark.

"Looking for a pretty teacher with freckles. Know anyone like that?"

She laughed, and the sensation felt wonderful. She'd been tense, listening to Don's story and reliving her own pitiful drama. She thanked God he'd tuned her thoughts back to reality. Her hang-ups were of her own making. Now, the challenge was to dump them.

"Don't know a soul like that," she said, stepping toward Mark. "So tell me. Why are you here. . .really?"

"I thought you'd enjoy a friendly face." He stepped into the room and sat on the edge of a student desk, looking around the room. "So this is where you pour knowledge into youthful minds."

"I try," she said.

"And today's your last day until fall?"

She lifted her pack of papers and grades. "Right here. I turn this in, and it's sweet freedom."

"You looked a little thoughtful when I watched you from the door," he said, his sensitive face acknowledging his suspicion.

"I had to deal with a problem today. It made me think." She told him briefly about Don's situation, but not her revelation. She'd hang on to that in private and see what she could do about the problems alone.

Mark stepped to her side and ran his fingers along the tense cords in her neck. "That was a great suggestion. I'm glad you invited him to come to church. . .especially when he lives so near."

"I don't know if he'll come, but I tried." She touched Mark's arm. "You know what was strange? Something you said awhile back came to me out of the sky. The words were perfect. It was almost as if—"

"As if God put them in your head?" He smiled at her and drew the palm of his hand down her back.

She nodded, awed at the realization. "Now that we're

being truthful," she said, sending him a knowing look, "tell me the real reason you came." He had something on his mind. She knew it in the pit of her empty stomach. "I'm waiting," she said, trying to sound blithe.

"I have a youth outing tomorrow morning, and my female chaperone broke her arm."

She eyed him suspiciously. "And who was this female chaperone?"

"Teri Dolan's mother. She tripped over the dog and fell on her right arm."

"And she can't chaperone with only one arm?"

He shook his head. "Not this activity. I need someone to volunteer."

The words, "Not this activity," made her nervous. "I'll pray that you find someone," Lana said with wide-eyed innocence.

He chuckled and touched her skin, letting his finger trail along her arm. "I always appreciate prayer, but today, I'd really appreciate a volunteer too."

"Would you like me to ask Barb?"

His eyes narrowed to a toying scowl, and he didn't respond.

"Oh, I see, you want me to volunteer." She quieted her heart, fighting the desire to yield to his charm. "I empathize, but my vacation starts tomorrow. During the school year, I'm knee-deep in teenagers. I couldn't bear to spend one more minute with. . ."

She broke off the sentence as his gaze caught her eyes.

"What's your outing? Not bowling, I hope." She tried to bite her tongue, but the words spilled out.

"Not bowling, I promise." A sly grin slid to his face. "Horseback riding."

That did it. She flung her palm forward like a policeman stopping traffic. "Not me. No way. Not on a horse. Carousel, maybe. But not a live horse that gallops and snorts."

"Have you ever been horseback riding? These horses lumber and plod. Trust me." He patted her arm. "Please, I'm desperate.

I'm new at this job. I can't take a mixed group of teens on an outing without at least one adult woman chaperone. You know that. And if I cancel, the kids will be so disappointed, not to mention their parents. I hate to start out on the wrong foot."

"I'm sure you can find someone else. Another parent or. . . someone." When she looked at his face, a sinking feeling washed over her.

"I don't know that many parents yet, and I hate to show defeat and bother Pastor Phil with this." He rested his hand on her arm. "Be a pal. I know you don't owe me anything. You've paid your debt." He sent her a beguiling smile. "Please come along. It's only a few hours."

Lana understood he was in a spot. But horseback riding? She and horses didn't speak the same language—or move in the same rhythm for that matter. She'd watched Westerns for years and noticed the smooth, elegant gate attained by horse and rider. The two times she'd had enough courage to climb—and she really meant climb—on a horse's back, she'd felt like the old Scottish folk song, "You take the high road, and I'll take the low road. And I'll get to Scotland afore ye." She went up and the horse went down, and the pain caused when they met in the middle was something she didn't want to remember.

But she looked into Mark's pleading eyes, and her mouth spoke without her brain participating. "All right, but this is the last time."

"Thanks a million," he said, drawing her into a bear hug. "We're leaving about nine. I'll stop by, and you can ride over with me."

"Okay," she said, feeling her cheek quiver like someone facing a firing squad.

"Now what can I do to repay you? Name it. I'm yours."

His spirited smile sent her heart flying, but her inner beast came out of hiding. She had a plan. "You're mine? Do you mean that?"

"Sure."

"How do you like to paint?"

"Paint? You mean—" He studied her face, his enthusiasm fading.

"Not by numbers; that's for sure" she said, enjoying his agony. "Walls. Lots of walls. Maybe even ceilings."

"Walls and ceilings," he repeated.

"That's right, and thanks," she said, allowing her finger to ramble playfully up his arm in the same way he'd captivated hers. "I'm so pleased you've volunteered for my project."

❧

Mark stepped from the car but didn't have to go far. Lana came out the side door dressed in jeans and a knit top. He noticed her sturdy hiking shoes and felt gratified that she at least knew how to dress for horseback riding.

"Good morning," he said, expecting her to respond, "What's good about it?"

Instead she yawned. "Good morning."

He grinned, pleased at her attitude. "I'm sure it feels nice being on vacation."

She sent him one of her looks. "My first day off, and I had to get up at the same time I always do."

"Sorry," he said, opening her door and watching her climb in. "But think of the good deed you're doing."

She arched one of her eyebrows and remained silent.

Relieved, Mark saw the hint of a smile flash for a heartbeat and knew she was teasing.

Leaning against the headrest, she closed her eyes, and Mark let her relax. She'd have a workout, he knew, but he appreciated her pinch-hitting. He'd wanted to ask her to come along from the beginning, but he'd watched her misery bowling and had decided to give her a break. Instead, Mrs. Dolan had experienced a break. . .a real one.

At the church, Lana stayed in the car while Mark made sure his fourteen charges were seat belted up with licensed drivers.

He set the ground rules, prayed with the teens, and climbed back into his car, relieved that he had enough teens to drive so he could make the trip with only Lana in his car.

They drove like a caravan, Mark leading the way, and when they parked at the stable, he steered them toward the building where men were saddling horses.

"I'm Mark Branson," he said to the dude in the cowboy hat. "I called last week. Fourteen teenagers and two adults." He eyed Lana and realized she looked as young as the kids.

The ranch hand only grunted and waved his arm toward the horses waiting to be mounted.

"This way." Mark beckoned to the group, and they followed, each attaching themselves to a horse as the stable crew gave them the animal's name and helped them mount.

Mark returned to Lana, hoping he could encourage a little enthusiasm. "I'll tell them to make sure they give you a mild-mannered mare." He slipped his arm around her shoulders and gave her a squeeze.

"Mild-mannered? Listen to that guy," she said. "Those plow horses have names. Charger, Buck, Titan, Cyclone, Gringo. Let me know when he comes to Sleepy, Dopey, or Bashful. That's my kind of horse."

"Don't worry," Mark said, patting her shoulder. "They give them spirited names to give the riders a thrill. They can go home and tell their friends they spent the day riding Avenger. Sounds more exciting than Daisy."

"You think so? Give me Daisy or Dandelion any day."

"Notice I said it sounds exciting." Mark tried to read her expression. At this point he wasn't sure if she were joking or serious, but either way he should have been more thoughtful and asked Pastor Phil to help him find a volunteer. If he really cared about her, he'd been stupid to force her to come along. . . even though he enjoyed her company. Why couldn't he stop being like his father, trying to push everyone into doing what he wanted?

Mark looked at Lana's tense face and hoped to ease her worry. "These poor animals have been up and down these paths so often they don't have to think. But it's fun for the kids. So here we are."

When the time came for her to mount, he followed Lana to the horse. "This one's docile, I hope," he murmured to the stable hand.

The man with the cowboy hat gave him a peculiar look and nodded.

Mark felt foolish asking the question, but he wanted Lana to feel secure. He boosted her up, and she managed to swing her short leg over the horse's rear. She grabbed the reins looking like he'd asked her to ride a bucking bronco. She towered above him, and he tipped his imaginary hat. "I'll be up on your level in a jiffy," he said, slipping his foot into his saddle's stirrup and swinging his leg over the saddle. "Nice weather up here."

"Are you kidding? Nothing's nice up here." She sent him a faint grin.

He patted the horse's mane. "Howdy, Fancy. You and I are going to be pals for an hour or so."

"Fancy?" Lana gave him and the horse a dubious look. "What kind of a name is that? Did you hear what they called my horse? If I need to plead with him, I'd like to address him by his first name.

Mark chuckled and tried to remember what the cowboy had mumbled. "Furry, I think. Sounds tame."

"Furry? That sounds like something they'd name a gerbil."

He grinned and looked ahead at the other riders. "Looks like they're moving out," Mark said, watching the dude with the cowboy hat wave them onto the trail. "Hang on."

six

Hang on? Lana sent Mark a look with the power to turn a dew glistening grape into a raisin. *Hang on!* That's what she had been doing. And tight.

Feeling the shift and sway of the horse's back, Lana watched the teens ahead of her as they plodded toward the wooded path. Fat-rumped horses lumbered along, their reeking odor growing stronger in the morning sunlight.

Mark rode beside her, looking comfortable and tall in the saddle. His blond hair glinted like gold in the sunlight, and his friendly eyes sparkled even brighter.

With the clip-clop of the horse's hooves, a peculiar urge rose in Lana to sing some sentimental western song, like "Get Along Little Doggies" or "Tumbling Tumbleweed." Instead the words, "Don't bury me on the lone prairie," intruded into her thoughts, barging through her mind like a guitar-strumming posse.

The teens had moved ahead down the shadowed path, and though she'd moaned about the horseback riding, she enjoyed the quiet of the woods. Bird songs and the snap of twigs beneath the horse's hooves sounded crisp and friendly in the dappled sunlight.

"We'd better catch up," Mark said, coaxing his steed into a trot.

As he bounced forward, Lana stayed behind, clinging to the reins and avoiding giving even the flick of motivation against her horse's back. Her caution was unwarranted. Furry and Fancy must have had a thing for each other, because Furry didn't want to be left behind. He shifted into passing gear, and the horse and Lana flew past Mark at a ragged clip—her up, the horse down, and then the painful meeting in the middle.

As she tugged on the reins, Mark caught up with her. "Sorry, Lana. Usually these old nags barely move."

"Furry's spurred on by the smell of my perfume, I think," she said, grasping for any comic relief she could muster. "And I'd give a lot for one whiff of eau d'cologne instead of the whiff I'm getting."

A grin stretched across Mark's face. "Just know that you're a lifesaver. The kids are having fun, and I think these first outings will bring them closer together so we have a friendly, cohesive group for summer camp."

"Summer camp?" Her chest vibrated with each step as she smacked against the ironclad leather beneath her and felt the chafing of the horse's ballooned sides against her legs.

"Church camp. It's the first time our church will have camp for the youth. I think it's a great way for teens to learn about nature, themselves, and God. Camping knits people together. They'll have memories they'll never forget."

She understood exactly what he meant. Her experience on this horse's back would cling to her memory like chewed gum to a shoe. Her bones rattled with each clop. "This horse and I aren't in sync. I think I've jarred my teeth loose," Lana said, wishing for a bathtub filled with warm, soothing, bubbly water.

"Gallops are natural and easier. Let's try."

Before she could protest, Mark dug his heels into Fancy's sides, and with the flick of the reins, he was off. Lana grabbed hold, knowing that Furry wasn't about to be outdone.

Sure enough, Furry gave a snort, and Lana sailed past Mark, clinging to the reins with one hand and the saddle horn with the other, but Mark had been right. She and the animal moved with the same up-down motion, and the ride would have been exhilarating except Lana realized that somehow the saddle hadn't been tightened properly. She felt herself slipping sideways. Seeing the woods from a vantage point parallel to the ground had not been part of the deal. She clung to the horse's scruffy mane for dear life, praying the saddle would stay put.

She'd caught up with the teens, but Furry had the zeal of a winner and had no plans to let another horse get in the way of the winner's circle.

With the thud of hooves and her beating heart, Lana galloped past a group of teens.

"Look at her go," Dennis called out.

"No fair," Susan grumbled. "How come she gets the best horse?"

An old adage with a new twist careened through Lana's thoughts. "Best is in the eye of the beholder," she yelled into the air. She would have willingly traded horses with the girl and thrown in a twenty-dollar bill to boot.

No more complaints met her ears, only a pitiful titter as she struggled to stay mounted. For the first time in her life, she understood the true meaning of sidesaddle.

About the time she thought she could bear no more, the path turned, and to her relief, the stables loomed straight ahead. But as Lana uttered a grateful sigh, Furry spotted the stable too. Apparently ready for lunch and a nap, the horse gave a resounding snort and whinny, then seemingly sprouted wings and bolted forward with momentum just short of a Concorde's.

"Look at Miss West," Gary echoed behind her. "I wish I was riding Fury."

Fury? Her heart rose to her throat. She distinctly remembered Mark calling the brute Furry. And forget the well-worn path. Whether Furry or Fury, she and the steed left the others eating dust. As they flew across the field, her life ripped past in fast-forward.

The horse stopped before she did, and when woman and

beast finally focused on each other, face-to-face, Lana found herself sprawled in his dinner on the floor of a stall.

Mark tore in behind her, waving his arms in panic. "Are you okay?" He stood over her, his face pale and pinched with concern. When he saw she had survived, his fear shifted gears to the familiar laugh that she'd grown to know too well.

"Put a muzzle on it," she said, rising to her feet and pulling straw from her hair. "Or you'll be eating this stuff."

She lifted an eyebrow, but the picture was too much even for her. Lana's laughter joined Mark's, and as she walked away from the stable, she had to admit her backside hurt much worse than her pride.

✧

By Monday, Lana could move her stiff, sore legs with greater agility. The "horse-side" ride, an apt name, lingered in her thoughts like an abscessed tooth. Yet if she were to admit it, the time spent with Mark gave the outing its pleasurable moments.

When the doorbell rang after dinner, she eased herself off the chair and went to the door. Mark stood on the porch with a sheepish grin and a bouquet of flowers.

"I should have gotten these to you earlier." He thrust his flower-laden hand toward her. "Accept these with my deep thanks and condolences." He made a gallant bow.

Lana grinned and swung the screen door open. "You look too humble. It doesn't suit you at all. Come on in."

He stepped past her into the foyer, and she swung the front door closed against the hot sunlight. Turning, she eyed his broad chest and recalled how handsome he looked on horseback. And how tender he'd been after his laughter had subsided.

She buried her nose in the bouquet, then looked into his eyes. The sparkle gave her heart a flutter, and she turned away before admiration rose to her face. "Let me get these in water."

"Good idea." His voice rang with playfulness behind her.

"You can have a seat." She motioned toward the living

room and continued her journey to the kitchen.

Opening a cabinet, she pulled out a vase and filled it with water. She unwrapped the florist paper and drew out the baby's breath from the bouquet. Touched by Mark's lovely gift, she nested their stems into water, then added the miniature carnations, daisies, and lilies.

"Looks good," he said.

She turned and found him standing in the doorway. "Thanks. They're beautiful."

"Not as pretty as you, though," he said, his gaze riveted to hers.

Startled by his comment, she faltered for a moment before finding something to say. "Now I know you're trying to wheedle me into something."

He smiled, but she feared she saw disappointment in his eyes. Trying to repair the damage, Lana carried the bouquet to him and tiptoed to kiss his cheek. "Thanks. I haven't had anyone give me flowers since. . . See? I can't even remember the last time."

He rested his palm on her arm. "You're more than welcome."

"I'll put them on the table," she said, beckoning him into the living room.

He followed her and plopped his tall frame into an easy chair, then stretched his legs out in front of him. "How are you feeling? I notice the limp is fading."

She sank onto the sofa. "My hobble's disappearing but not the memory. I've ended my cowgirl career. Not even your pleading tears will ever move me to agree to a venture like that again."

He squirmed with a grin. "How are you with canoes?"

Her head zoomed upward. "Why?" She narrowed her eyes, hoping the look pinned him to the chair.

"Just making conversation." A wry look filtered across his face.

Her stomach tightened. "Like pig's wings. Tell me the truth." Gazing into his face, she felt herself weakening—with or without his pleading.

"I'm teasing." He leaned forward, elbows on his knees. "I'm working on the Christian camp activities. I think it will be fun."

"Some people's idea of fun isn't healthy," she said, enjoying his puzzled expression.

"But camping is. Fresh air, nature, exercise, and God."

"Great. I had my rebuttal planned, but you ruined it. How can I say anything negative when you included the Lord in your list?" She folded her arms across her chest.

"I know you can't. That was my plan."

She unfolded her arms and sent him a sweet smile. "Want to know my plan? What I've been thinking about—while sitting here wounded and in misery?"

"Okay. What?" he asked, rising and sliding next to her on the sofa. "Tell me. Maybe it's the same thing that's on my mind."

She caught an innuendo in his comment, and it rattled her. She liked him—a lot. But Mark seemed too perfect for her. Too optimistic. Too expecting. He presumed she experienced his enthusiasm for life and his penchant for helping others. On the other hand, life did seem more exciting when he was around.

"Why so quiet?" he asked.

"I'm thinking about what might be on your mind, because I doubt if it's paint and wallpaper."

He collapsed against the sofa back and groaned. "You mean you haven't forgotten that project?"

"I haven't forgotten the project or your offer." She moved her face closer to his and looked him straight in the eyes. "I believe it went something like, 'Name it. I'm yours.' "

He inhaled, and the zesty scent of mint filled the space between them.

"I recall hearing someone say that." He pressed his palm against her cheek. "You don't really want me to paint. I'll drip the stuff all over the place."

Flustered by his closeness, she eased away. "I use drop cloths. No problem."

"I suppose I owe you this," he said, standing and eyeing the walls. "Are we painting this room? It looks good to me."

"No. The dining room and my bedroom. . .plus I'm doing stenciling in there." She rose and showed him the decorating plans she had for the summer. "And I want to buy border for the dining room to go around at the height where you usually find chair molding."

"Okay. I give. You're about as manipulative as I am."

Lana grabbed his waist from behind and guided him into the kitchen. "Hungry?"

He turned and faced her. "Starving, but I want to take you out to dinner for a change."

"Don't trust me?" she asked.

"Sure I do, but the flowers were only part of my apology." He shook his head, his face earnest. "When I saw you sprawled out on the stable floor, I—" His laugh started with a chuckle.

"You laughed. I know." She poked him in the ribs. "So listen here, Mr. Nice Guy. Not only do you buy me dinner, but we're picking out paint samples. Maybe even the border."

"A–all that for a little. . .laughter?" he sputtered.

Lana gave him a nudge. "He who laughs last, laughs best. You'd better remember that."

❧

Music spilled out into the air as Lana climbed the steps to the church entrance. Since Barb lagged behind, Lana didn't wait and headed inside. She'd missed church the previous Sunday, unable to sit on the hard pews, and now she dreaded to face the teens who'd watched her make her sidesaddle debut on a horse named Fury.

When she entered the vestibule, Mark waited for her and waved in greeting.

"The kids have been asking about you," he said.

"Did you tell them I survived the ordeal with minimal scars?"

He hooked his arm through hers. "I told them you were wonderful. Do you mind if I sit with you?"

She scanned the congregation, wondering what people might say. "If you think you can deal with the gossip."

"No gossip in here. It's a sin." With a grin, he released her arm but walked beside her to the middle of the sanctuary, then motioned her into a row.

"Keep an eye out for Barb." Lana turned, looking over her shoulder for her sister. She spotted her a few rows back, seated with a man Lana didn't know. She turned back to Mark. "Never mind," she whispered, "she's with a friend." Playfully, she wiggled her eyebrows.

"Really? Let me check him out." Mark glanced behind him.

Lana shifted and gave another subtle glance, but instead, her eyes focused on a young man sliding into a back pew. She swung back toward Mark. "The boy from my class is here. The one I invited to visit the church. Remember? Don Fabrizio."

"He is? Where?" He twisted in the seat and glanced over his shoulder.

She turned again. "In the third row from the back. He's wearing a blue knit shirt."

"I wonder if I should send one of the kids over to sit with him." He shifted and faced the front. "I could probably ask Gary."

"I don't think so. Don might feel uncomfortable. Let's wait until after the service."

As Mark nodded, the organ began the introduction, and they rose to sing the first hymn.

As the service continued, Lana wondered how Don felt

worshiping alone in an unfamiliar church. She didn't want to turn around so she kept her eyes forward, but her thoughts stayed with the young man. When Pastor Phil rose and began his sermon, Lana's pulse heightened as she listened to the verses he read from Ezekiel 18:

> The word of the Lord came to me: "What do you people mean by quoting this proverb about the land of Israel:
> " 'The fathers eat sour grapes, and the children's teeth are set on edge'?
> "As surely as I live, declares the Sovereign Lord, you will no longer quote this proverb in Israel. For every living soul belongs to me, the father as well as the son—both alike belong to me. The soul who sins is the one who will die."

Pastor Phil laid his Bible down and looked at the congregation. "Today we will focus on what God expects of us. In these verses, we learn that we must learn to follow Jesus' call without worrying about our family's failings. We do not take on the sins of our father. What we do is follow Jesus and let Him rule our lives."

Lana let the words wash over her. She knew God's Word could give Don hope. He could throw off the weight of his father's sin. His task was to follow Jesus. But could the teenager do that? Her own past dragged through her mind. How long had she tried to prove herself to the world to make herself worthy of the gifts she received just as she struggled to show her father appreciation? But her gratitude now was not to a single person or the world. She had nothing to prove and would never be worthy except by the grace of God through Jesus.

Bathed in that thought, she settled back and prayed Don had also been touched by the message. She felt Mark's hand resting beside hers on the pew. She longed to cover it with her palm, to feel his pulse beating beneath her fingers, but she pushed the thought away.

They rose for the last hymn, and when the service ended, Lana clutched Mark's arm and hurried them through the departing worshipers to reach Don. "Hello," she said, grasping the young man's arm. "I'm so glad you came."

"I–I surprised myself," he said. "I woke up this morning, and something made me get up early. Next thing I know, I'm walking to church."

Lana gave Mark a knowing look, recognizing how God had worked in the teenager's life. She grasped his arm. "Don, this is Mark Branson, the youth director I told you about."

"Hi," Mark said. "I'm pleased you accepted Miss West's invitation." He extended his hand, and the young man grasped it in a firm shake.

"Like I said, I surprised myself," Don said. He shifted his eyes toward a group of teens as if looking for someone his age.

Lana gave Mark a desperate look.

Thinking quickly, he flagged one of the nearby teens, and Gary joined him with a smile.

"Hi, Don," Gary said. "What are you doing here?"

Mark chuckled. "Same as you probably. Worshiping the Lord."

Gary looked embarrassed. "I knew that. I meant I've never seen you here before," he said, addressing Don.

"Miss West suggested I visit some Sunday." He tucked his hands in his pocket and lowered his eyes. "And here I am."

"Glad you're here," Gary said. "Hey, what about tonight? We're having a planning meeting for summer camp, but it's a pizza party too. What do you say?"

Don grinned. "Pizza sounds good."

"And the church pays for it," Mark added. "That makes it extra special." He gave Don's arm a friendly shake. "After our meeting, we usually have a Bible study."

Don nodded. "I have a Bible."

"Then bring it along," Lana added.

"Will you be there, Miss West?"

She wanted to sink into the ground. "Well. . .I. . ." Mark's gaze riveted to her face, and she read the message in his eyes. "I–I'll be there. Sure."

Mark's hand slipped to her arm and gave it a squeeze.

Somehow either Mark or God or both were involving her in things she had no intention of doing—just like Barb had done over the past years. Lana paused, letting the thought wash over her. She was strong willed and purposeful. If she really didn't want to do these things, why would she agree? Had she been led because that's what she wanted to do in her heart all along?

seven

Lana plucked a pepperoni from her pizza wedge and dropped it into her mouth, enjoying the spicy tang. She chewed and swallowed, then took a full bite of pizza. The zesty sauce and rich creamy cheese lay on her tongue, and she licked her lips to capture every morsel.

"Good, isn't it?" Don said, sitting beside her.

"Sure is," she said, watching Don's expression as he chowed down a large slice.

"We don't get pizza at home," he said. "My dad wants meat and potatoes."

"Then this is a treat," she added, not wanting to say more in earshot of other teens.

He nodded.

Although Don seemed a little uneasy, the kids he knew from school had been sociable and welcoming. Lana prayed this would be only the beginning for her student.

The pizza vanished quickly, and while Lana cleared up the boxes and paper plates, Mark started the meeting. She heard only snatches of the conversation, and when she settled down with the group, they had turned to the topic of the camping trip's purpose.

Dressed in khakis and a blue-and-beige knit top, Mark stood beside a podium and addressed the teens with his usual patience and good nature. "Sure, camp is for having fun," he said, obviously not wanting to embarrass the girl who'd offered fun as the trip's purpose, "but besides fun, what else can we accomplish?"

Like any classroom, the answers varied—exercise, a good

tan, appreciation for home cooking—but eventually more serious answers evolved.

"Friendship," Gary said.

"Good answer," Mark said, focusing on Gary. "What do you mean by friendship?"

The teen scowled, appearing uncertain how to respond. "Well, getting to know each other better."

"And care about the other campers," Teri said.

"We'll learn things we have in common," Jason called out.

"Great," Mark said, smiling as the answers flew. "Anything else?"

"Learning new things," Don said, "you know. . .like archery maybe."

Mark nodded.

"Or canoeing."

"And canoeing helps us learn something else." Mark looked over the faces and grinned. "How about cooperation?"

"Right," Gary said. "You can't canoe without that."

"So we can learn cooperation. What else?" Mark asked.

"Compromise," Lana added. "How to split the difference."

A quirky grin appeared on his face. "Miss West is right. Sometimes we have to know when to give a little."

"Cooperation means teamwork," Susan added.

"Now we're getting somewhere," Mark said, "because teamwork is one of our major focuses on our trip. Think about teamwork. What's part of teamwork? We've already mentioned cooperation and compromise. How about another C word? Communication."

"You can't cooperate if you don't communicate," Dennis called out.

"Excellent. You're right. If we don't communicate, nothing happens. We're at a standstill."

"Trust," Don said. "We have to trust people to do their part when we work as a team. . .like in football."

"That's so true, Don. Trust is a vital factor in all kinds of relationships—employer-employee, child-parent, romance, marriage, and God."

"How will we learn about trust at camp?" Susan asked.

Mark laughed. "That's my surprise. You can expect a lot of challenges as well as a lot of fun."

"And a lot of learning," Lana added, thinking about the types of activities Mark might use to teach the teens teamwork. . .and trust.

Mark pulled a Bible from beneath the podium. "Speaking of trust, let's take a look at God's Word. Do you all have Bibles? If not, share. Okay?"

Shuffles and murmurs rattled in the air while they opened their Bibles and agreed who would share with whom. Having heard about the Bible study, Lana had brought hers along and waited for Mark's direction. When a hush settled over the crowd, Mark began.

"Open the Scripture to Matthew 11:28. Follow along with me: 'Come to me, all you who are weary and burdened, and I will give you rest. Take my yoke upon you and learn from me, for I am gentle and humble in heart, and you will find rest for your souls. For my yoke is easy and my burden is light.' " He stood a moment looking out over the teens. "What does Jesus mean in these verses?"

A hush settled over the room, and Lana watched the teens' faces, twisted with bewilderment or eyes lowered to avoid being called upon. As always, Mark waited with patience. Lana filled with admiration. He had a way with young people—not a friend exactly, but like a counselor, probing and challenging, but without judgment.

When Lana could no longer bear the silence and wanted to send out a response herself, a girl raised her hand, and Mark nodded toward her.

"I understand the easy part," she said. "Jesus invites us to give our problems to Him rather than try to handle them all by ourselves."

Mark nodded and sent the girl a smile.

Silence weighed on the room.

Lana noticed Don squirming as if wanting to speak. Finally, he lifted his hand, and Mark gave him a nod.

"I'm not sure I understand that second part," he said. "The part about take my yoke on you." A frown settled on his face. "A yoke is like a harness that holds two oxen together, right?"

"That's right," Mark said. "Oxen or any draft animal. Horses too."

"So Jesus isn't just telling us to dump our problems on Him and split."

When the group giggled, Lana cringed, fearing Don would be offended, but Don grinned along with them.

Mark pushed the subject forward. "What is Jesus telling us, Don?"

"That He'll share the weight of our problems?" His face filled with anxiety.

Mark gave him a thumbs up. "Absolutely, Don."

The teen's expression switched to pleasure.

"Okay, someone else answer this," Mark said. "What's the problem with sharing the weight of a heavy load with someone?"

Murmurs rose from the teens, but no one responded.

"It's teamwork, right? You need to communicate," Mark said, prodding them to think.

"Don't you need to trust that someone's carrying their half of the load?" Gary asked.

"Aha. We're back to trust again," Mark said. "That's right, Gary."

Lana listened to the discussion on trust and thought about her own trust issues. Was she so afraid to trust others she had to be in charge to make sure the job was done right? Did she look at God's promises in the same way? Why would God be willing to bear her burdens?

Her thoughts drifted to her own petite stature. Too short. Too unsubstantial. So many things she couldn't carry or reach by herself. Family and friends always had to pitch in and help her. She realized Jesus made the same promise but about things that were bigger and more serious. He offered to bear the load and give His children rest.

By the time she'd tuned back into the conversation, the topic had shifted from trust to summer camp. The students raised questions, and Mark shot back answers.

"We'll have at least two parent chaperones. Maybe three," Mark said. "Each of them will be responsible for a cabin."

"You too?" Gary asked.

"Sure thing. I'll take a cabin."

"I want to be in Miss West's cabin," Susan said. "Okay?" She looked at Lana.

Lana sank into her chair, wishing she could vanish. After listening to their conversation on trust and cooperation, how could she tell the girl she had no interest in being a camp counselor?

Mark's amusement was blatant. A grin stretched across his face from sideburn to sideburn. "What do you say, Miss West?"

"Lana," she said. "I feel like someone's grandmother with the 'Miss West' tag."

The crowd hooted and laughed.

She'd avoided the answer, and the topic turned in another direction as she sighed with relief.

"I'll be calling a meeting with all of the parents so we can set down the ground rules," Mark said. "Any questions?"

Heads shook no, but Dennis asked if there was any more pizza. That line got another laugh, and finally, the group rose and began their trek to the door.

Lana stood off in the distance, fearing Susan might corner her again about being a camp counselor. When the last teen vanished through the doorway, Lana released a panicked gasp. She eyed Mark across the room, a smile still brightening his face.

"Trapped," he said. "I saw you squirm. The kids want you to come along."

"No way. I have teens under my feet all year, remember? And I hate camping."

"Teens under your feet all year means you're skilled. Don't forget, you have two weeks to get prepared."

"Prepared?" She crumpled into a folding chair. "What about my paint and wallpaper?"

"You've got me. I'm your handy-dandy painter man. We'll have that job licked before we leave."

Looking at his kind face and good-humored smile, her arguments sounded weak. "But I detest sleeping bags and bugs. Not to mention snakes."

"I won't mention them—not once. Promise." He crossed his heart with his index finger. "The job's not bad," he added, his voice soft and convincing. "You'd only have to sleep in the cabin to keep an eye on them and help with a couple group activities. That's it. No horses. I promise. The rest of the time you'd be on your own. Like a mini-vacation."

"About as mini as you can get." She disliked camping and bugs more than she could say, but the look in his tender eyes tugged at her heart. He was all a woman could want—sweet, funny, handsome, and truly filled with the fruit of the Spirit. She liked that.

"What are you thinking?" he asked.

She felt her frozen determination thawing.

He didn't push her, but waited, his patience overwhelming. He fiddled with his cuticle, giving her an occasional cursory glance as if too much motion would refreeze her block of resolve.

As her resistance puddled at her feet, she turned to soft

mush. "How long is the stay at camp?"

His head triggered upward. "Two weeks."

"Two weeks." The words rumbled from her in a moan. "What happened to all the one-week camping trips?"

"No good for our purpose. Team-building, Bible study, and fun—two weeks works best. We'll leave on a Saturday and come back a week from the following Friday."

"You're making two weeks sound like a short time," she said, recognizing a con job when she saw one.

"I know, but think about this. Not only would I appreciate your coming along, the Lord will too."

"Did you ask Him?" She sent him a half-hearted grin. "Do you promise to never darken my door again with another request?"

A lengthy silence filled the room, and the look of guilt settled over his face. "I. . .I don't want to promise never. But how's this? I'll really try to never ask you for a favor like this again."

"That makes me feel much better."

His chuckle joined hers. And though she hadn't agreed, they both knew she'd go.

☙

Mark climbed down the ladder, then examined the ceiling. It looked good to him, but he was also aware of Lana's high expectations. Good to him and good to her could mean two different things. "What do you think?" he asked as he rested his brush across the edge of the paint can.

Lana turned toward him, and when he saw her face, an amused grin tugged at his mouth.

"What?" she asked. Her eyes narrowed, and her head tilted at a questioning angle.

"The ceiling." He looked upward, admiring his work. "What do you think?"

She gave her head a quick shake. "Not that. What's the silly smile for?"

"One thing at a time," he said, closing the distance between them. He guided her head upward. "The ceiling? Good or bad?"

"The ceiling looks great." She tugged her chin to its normal position. "Now, why the grin?"

He touched her cheek. "The war paint. It looks great on you. . .but then, most things do."

The feel of her soft, warm skin sent a sweet sensation down his arm, and his pulse did an unexpected jog.

"War paint?" She fingered her cheek and backed away through the dining-room doorway.

Mark watched her go, grinning at the splotch of hunter green latex on her cheek. He moved the ladder and eyed the can of paint the color he'd admired on Lana's face. She had a long way to go to finish the walls. He needed to wash his brush and join her on that project.

In a moment, Lana returned, the paint splotch missing. Where it had been, only a rosy tinge remained, evidence of her vigorous scrubbing.

"Too bad," he said. "You look good in green."

"So will you. . .when I pour this can over your head." She sent him a teasing smile.

"Before I tackle the walls with you, how about a break?"

She glanced at her hands, now clean from her face scrubbing. "I suppose. . .before I'm speckled again."

Mark wiped the rim of his paint can with a rag, then tapped the lid onto the can with a rubber mallet. Lana did the same with the green latex, then straightened and headed for the kitchen.

"Want a sandwich?" she asked over her shoulder.

"Sure," he said, surveying his painting clothes before he settled into a wooden kitchen chair.

After swinging open the refrigerator door, Lana pulled open the meat drawer and lifted out ham slices and a wrapper of cheese.

"Can I help?" Mark asked, standing up. Lana handed him

the packages, which he placed on the table, and as she pulled out lettuce and condiments, Mark got down two plates from the cabinet.

Lana poured iced tea into glasses, tore open a bag of chips, and settled at the table across from Mark.

He concentrated on building a sandwich, and after the blessing, he took a bite, enjoying the blend of meat and cheese. . . but even more Lana's company. He wondered if she felt the same. Her face looked content and relaxed, and lately Mark sensed they had both grown comfortable with each other.

"Thanks for helping me with this project," Lana said. "Ceilings are so difficult for me."

"I'm enjoying the challenge." Mark dropped a few potato chips onto his plate. "And you've certainly gone the extra miles for me and the teens."

She sat a moment in silence, her lips pursed in thought. "Odd you mention me and the kids. I've been giving that some thought myself."

"What? Going the extra mile?" And she truly had when he considered bowling, horseback riding, the meeting, and now her silent agreement to be a camp chaperone. The whole transition amazed him, and he definitely saw God's hand working the miracle.

"That too, but. . .no, it's more than that." Her gaze lowered, and she stared at her plate a moment before looking up. "I'm really enjoying the kids at the church. Maybe the difference is that it's not my job. I'm not responsible for hammering knowledge into their heads. At the pizza meeting the other night, did you hear them?"

"Sure. . .but what do you mean exactly?" The comment stirred individual responses in his head—Gary, Susan, and the new boy Don.

Her eyes widened. "They were thinking." She pushed a strand of hair behind her ear. "Sure, you prodded a little, but they were expressing ideas on their own. And even better, they showed interest and asked meaningful questions. Why can't I teach like that?"

"Don't get down on yourself," Mark said, letting his hand slide across the table to capture hers. "We were dealing with a topic close to their hearts—the Lord and their relationships to Him and to each other. I wasn't trying to get them to put a comma in the right place or remember who was at the Alamo and what happened there."

"I suppose," she said, a thoughtful frown settling on her face. "I was so pleased when Don jumped in with his comments, and then I felt terrible when the kids laughed at him."

"Not at him. With him. There's a big difference, and laughter is a wonderful medicine. Do you realize how much healing takes place when we can laugh at our own failings and problems?"

She nodded, and a faint grin curved her lips. "Lately, I've had to admit some of my own ridiculous idiosyncrasies."

He squeezed her hand and longed to carry it to his lips and kiss the soft, smooth flesh that left him feeling addled. "They're not ridiculous. Not at all. Those qualities are what makes you you. They make you dear to my heart. They make me smile."

"So. . .you're laughing at me," she said, a lovely glow brightening her face.

"Laughing at humanity. What about my foolishness?" He winced waiting for her list.

"You aren't foolish at all."

Her response startled him. "Sure I am. What about making jokes all the time. . .even when I should give a serious answer? What about manipulating? Not the first time, but after that, I allowed things to progress, hoping to motivate you to come along with me and the teens. . .against your will."

"I don't know about that, Mark." She leaned forward and

rested her palm against his fingers. "I thought about that the other day. You know how bullheaded I am."

Teasing, he nodded with an extra measure of enthusiasm. Again he was taunting when he should have been serious.

"Don't overdo it," she said, shaking her head at his silliness. "I started thinking about my response to stimuli. If I'm so set on doing things my own way, then why am I allowing myself to be manipulated?" She lifted her thoughtful face and locked her gaze with his.

Mark considered what she'd said. Was she saying she chose to be maneuvered? Did she want someone to take charge and control her? He couldn't quite believe that. "Maybe you don't have the patience to fight off people's exploitation." Hating to admit the truth, he meant himself.

She chuckled. "Patience. Now that's another problem. No, I wonder if deep in my heart I know what is right and really want to be more thoughtful and generous. Maybe it's just difficult to change the way I've functioned for so long. Sort of a pride issue. Do you understand?"

"You mean you have to keep proving to the world that you're tough and you can do it your own way?" He eyed her, wondering if he'd hit anywhere near what she was thinking.

"Right. Something like that. God wants me to be humble and hear His will." She turned her attention to the sandwich, lifted it to her mouth, and took a bite.

Feeling almost as if she were talking about him, Mark let the conversation fade and concentrated on his lunch. Yet curious, he wondered if she were telling him she felt she had changed. Change seemed to sneak up on people. It did on him. . .that day at college registration he'd learned when God wanted to improve him, He didn't sound the trumpets. Things just changed.

Lana rose, slipping the final chip from her plate into her mouth and carried her dish to the sink.

After Mark finished his sandwich, he brushed the crumbs from the table to his plate, then followed her. Standing behind her at the sink, he let his gaze explore her petite frame, her slender arms busy beneath the tap, rinsing the dishes with a soapy sponge. He eyed an unruly strand of hair that wanted to be noticed, and on a whim, he lifted his finger and pushed it behind her ear. . .like she did so often.

She glanced at him over her shoulder, surprised yet smiling.

He longed to turn her around, to hold her in his arms and feel her slender body against his, but a warning harnessed his behavior. Let God's work continue in both of them. When the time seemed right, Mark would know in his heart—and most important, he would know God's will.

Instead of reacting as his heart desired, he lowered the dishes into the sink and backed away, wrapped in the scent of herbal shampoo and lemony dish soap. A prayer fluttered through his mind. *Keep my direction steady, heavenly Father, and guide me in the way that You want me to go. In Jesus' precious name.*

A sense of wholeness settled over him, and he followed Lana back to the dining room, readying to paint the walls while God coated his spirit with joy and insight.

⁂

A warm summer breeze filtered across Lana's arms and ruffled her hair. She lifted her fingers and pulled them through her short locks, catching a glimpse of herself in a storefront window. Her heart skipped a beat, eyeing Mark beside her, his broad shoulders and impressive height dwarfing her in the reflection.

Lately, she'd felt smaller than usual, but not just physically. The expanse of Mark's heart had knocked her down a peg. The knock had been her own doing. Mark's generosity and kindness would never allow him to belittle her, but she measured herself against him as a person and found herself humbled by the experience. No, she'd not become perfect, but she sensed an improvement for which she felt grateful.

"I hope we have nice weather like this at camp," Mark said. He'd gained a healthy looking tan while playing basketball and volleyball with the teens in the church yard after school, getting to know them better.

"Me too," Lana said. "I suppose we have to be prepared for everything."

Mark chuckled. "Not snow. But rain and cool evenings. Bring a sweatshirt and a poncho if you have one."

His helpful advice left Lana with less confidence about two weeks at camp, but she'd promised herself to focus on the bright side. "I have one."

She paused beside him at one of the few streetlights in town. While she waited, Mark's hand brushed hers, and to her delight, he wove his fingers through hers, giving her a hopeful glance.

Lana didn't hesitate, but tightened her grip to let him know she approved. She avoided looking at him for fear her emotions would show on her face. Instead, she kept her focus on the shop windows.

"Hungry?" Mark asked.

"Not really," she said, knowing the relationship she longed for couldn't be satisfied with food.

"How about some lemonade or maybe a dessert?"

"Lemonade sounds good," she said.

"Let's try the Holly Hotel," he suggested.

"Good idea. They might not be busy this time of day."

They crossed the street, and Lana ascended the steep steps, then waited while Mark opened the door to the historic hotel where Carrie Nation, the suffragette, had taken her axe to the hotel bar. Once inside, Lana admired the carved wainscoting and enjoyed the air-conditioning that cooled her arms. In a few minutes, the hostess seated them near the front windows covered with lace curtains that filtered the view of the street.

Lana declined dessert and sipped her lemonade while Mark dug into a slice of cheesecake with cherry sauce. She watched the red syrup escape the fork, and he licked his tongue across his lips, giving her a warm chuckle.

"I'm like a little kid. I can't stay away from the candy jar."

In her heart, Mark seemed far from a kid. He was all the man Lana wanted, even with his boyish behavior. She remained silent, enjoying the antique surroundings and the pleasant cool air while she watched him finish the dessert.

He pushed the plate aside and took a drink of iced tea. "I've been wanting to get your input," he said, leaning forward on his elbows, "about some of the team activities I could use. I have a couple ideas, but I thought you might have some others since you spend so much time with teenagers."

She shook her head. "I work in a classroom, and most of their activities are individual. They have group projects once in awhile, like a report or panel discussion, but that wouldn't work in a camp setting."

He remained silent, his eyes focused on the white linen tablecloth. "I'll need an ice breaker on our first night. Something fun, but an activity that needs cooperation."

"How about a scavenger hunt?" she suggested, remembering the parties she'd attended in her youth.

"No neighbors here. Don't they have to knock on doors and ask for things?"

"You could list items they can find in the woods. Better yet, make it like a road rally where they have to decipher puzzles to figure out where to look for the next clue."

"I've never been on one," he said. "Guess I've missed something."

She chuckled. "Nothing life shattering. Let's see. A clue could be hidden near the canoes. Then you need to set up clues to lead them to the canoe. You might have five questions that need answers, and each answer begins with one of the letters that will spell out the location of the next clue."

"That sounds confusing. Give me an example."

She sighed. "Okay, let's take the canoe idea. First question. What thing a day keeps the doctor away?"

"Apple."

"Right," she said. "That gives you the letter A. Now where are Christians on Sunday morning?"

"Church," he said.

"Now you have the A and C. They know they're looking for the first letter of each word. After five questions, they'll have all the letters spelling canoe, and they shift them around until they know where to look."

"I get it. So what do they find at the canoe?"

"At the canoe, you'll have another puzzle for each team to solve. Each team figures out the solutions at different times, so usually one team is already gone before another one arrives. Road rallies are fun."

"And what do they get at the end?"

"You'll have a prize for the winning group. A special treat or reward of some kind."

"I like it. Could I count on you to organize that one for me?"

He gave her one of his sweet smiles she couldn't resist, and he knew it.

"I'll see what I can do," she said.

"Thanks." He sipped the iced tea, his finger brushing away the condensation. "My goal is to teach them to trust and have faith in each other but also to learn that they can trust the Lord, confident His direction is unfailing."

His direction is unfailing. Lana considered Mark's words, knowing that she really needed to listen to God's instruction. She knew she was falling in love with Mark, but even if he loved her in return, could she offer him the support he needed or be the partner that God commanded her to be?

eight

Lana glanced out the rear window of Mark's car and saw the large bus bounding behind them. They'd left the main highway, and now the washboard road rattled Mark's newer model car like a pair of maracas. For once her small stature seemed a blessing since she'd noticed Mark's head occasionally smack the roof of the car when he hit the bigger potholes.

Lana felt her fast-food lunch flipping around in her stomach. "You'd think they'd grate this cow path, wouldn't you?" she asked.

"They probably don't want campers to get too hopeful," Mark said, rubbing the top of his head from the previous bump.

"Too hopeful about what?" Though she asked the question, fear settled into her well-shaken stomach.

"Not to expect too much luxury," he answered.

"But what about necessity? A car's axle is not what I'd call a luxury."

"Good point," he said as he hit another jarring hole. "Camps have low budgets, I suppose. Church camps are funded by congregations' generosity."

Lana shifted in her seat. "Let's pray that the First Church of Holly will become a generous donor."

He grinned and gripped the vibrating steering wheel.

Looking behind her, Lana spied the sway and bounce of the bus and felt grateful she'd been able to ride with Mark. Two parents had volunteered for bus duty, and Mark had said one car was needed for an emergency. Emergencies were now on Lana's thankful list.

97

"There it is," Mark said, pointing through the windshield off to the right.

Lana strained to see a group of smaller log cabins nestled in a wide semicircle beside a larger building. "That must be the office," she said.

"Office, cafeteria, game room, and meeting rooms, I imagine. I've been to a few camps in my day. They're all about the same."

But as they drew closer, Lana cringed. From a distance, the rustic cabins had looked truly rustic, which made her nervous. When they pulled into the camp grounds and stopped, "from a distance" had become the best view of her two-week accommodations.

She stepped from the car and watched the teens spill from the bus, carrying sleeping bags and duffel bags. The driver opened the rear and unloaded suitcases, boxes, and overnight bags.

While they gathered their belongings, Mark spoke to the camp director, and soon everyone had gathered to receive their cabin assignments. As the director called names and assigned a cabin, the campers moved to the side.

Lana waited for hers while one of the parents beckoned a group to follow her to a cabin called Running Deer. Another counselor herded a group toward Sleeping Bear. With her obvious inexperience, she feared her bunkhouse might be called Dying Hawk or Wounded Possum, but she smiled when she heard her cabin assignment: Little Flower. Now that name she liked. In moments, Mark led his crew across the grass toward Soaring Eagle, and Lana eyed the log cabin in the opposite direction and assumed it was hers.

When she stepped inside, a dank, mildew aroma greeted her, and Lana remembered Flower was the skunk's name in the children's tale *Bambi*. Grasping for optimism, she told herself that mildew was better than skunk smell any day.

As she peered at the log-walled room with only a narrow walkway between bunk beds, she questioned her sanity. Even a self-respecting mouse would avoid the drafty, damp interior for some cozy nest in a knothole.

Just like the rodent, Lana wished for such a sanctuary. Instead, she herded eight chattering teenage girls into a twenty-by-sixteen-foot space, no closets, and a makeshift nightstand void of even a candle, let alone a lamp. Five grimy windows and two glaring overhead bulbs served as the only sources of light.

Forcing her too large suitcase beneath her cot, Lana panicked. Where was the bathroom? With one door at the back and another at the front, the answer to her question did not seem promising. She folded her arms as a war cry sounded in her head. Mark had called this a mini-vacation with a wonderful natural setting. No bathroom was too natural for Lana. She darted outside, ready to wring Mark's neck.

The other cabin stood across a stretch of grass and dirt, and Mark stood outside herding in his charges. Catching his eye, she strode toward him, but he turned and appeared to be heading in the opposite direction. "Wait up, Mr. Youth Director," Lana called.

Mark stopped while Lana watched his grimace tug into a Cheshire Cat smile that didn't fool her. "I didn't know," he said before she could say a word.

Her fists jabbed against her waist. "You mean you didn't check the place out first?"

His arms flailed out from his sides. "I read their brochures. It sounded typical to me. Rustic cabins, sandy beaches, canoes, hiking, archery. What more could a person want?"

"How about walls without cracks, a lamp on the nightstands, a hook for clothes, and a door that leads somewhere other than outside."

Mark moved toward her and wrapped his arm around her

shoulders. "Sounds like you've never been camping."

She nodded her head voraciously, hoping he sensed her sarcasm. "You can say that again. And what about a restroom?"

"About fifty yards that way," he said, his finger aimed at a small, gray building. "I hope you remembered a flashlight."

She arched a brow. "And shower?"

His mouth curled to a sheepish grin. "The camp director said there's only one shower." Mark lifted a half-hearted finger toward another less-than-eye-catching building about one hundred yards away. "That means we need a schedule. Women shower at night and men in the morning."

"Dandy." She gave him her best evil eye.

Mark squeezed her shoulder reassuringly. "Hey, cheer up. Once you get into the spirit of it all, you'll think camping's fun. And things could be worse."

"They could? How?"

He tweaked her cheek and spun on his heel toward his own home-away-from-home. Before Lana took a step, a shriek pealed from her cabin. She raced back and met two teens exiting as she attempted to enter. "What happened?" she asked as she studied their ashen faces.

"A mouse. . .with wings," Susan screeched.

"Bats," Teri corrected her in a pitch that didn't sound as confident as her response.

Wrapping her arm around her hair—just in case—Lana darted inside. As she gaped toward the ceiling, she saw what had panicked the girls. A frightened bat had awakened from its rest in the rafters and was dive-bombing the bunks. Recalling her line about no self-respecting mouse, she realized she hadn't thought about a lowly bat. Apparently they didn't care at all where they lived.

But she did.

Though she wanted to be a good sport, a bat in her bunkhouse wasn't acceptable. She spun around and marched outside.

With one sweeping view of the area, she headed for a building marked "Camp Office." She would give them a piece of her mind—maybe two pieces while she felt in the mood.

෨

Mark looked around the quiet cabin and took a full breath. Along with the stale, damp odor, he smelled relief. He'd gotten his nine young men organized and sent them out to enjoy the scenery. The two parent counselors had finished setting up their cabins, and most everyone had drifted off in various directions.

Though the cabins were a disappointment, he'd spied the water and headed that way, praying he'd find the wide beach he'd admired in the brochure along with a few sturdy canoes and rowboats. Usually optimistic, he smiled when he saw the narrow sandy shoreline. At least one thing in the pamphlet appeared to be somewhat accurate. Canoes and a couple rowboats had been piled along the grassy bank, and he eyed them, looking for telltale holes. Seeing nothing but solid wood, his optimism grew. If they could survive the beyond-rustic cabins, the two weeks might prove to be enjoyable.

Already teens were sitting cross-legged in the grass, talking, while others waded through the cadet blue water. Some he'd seen heading in the opposite direction, he assumed to investigate the wooded paths and discover where they led.

Alone for a moment, Mark eased himself down on the grassy bank and stared across the sun-specked water. He hadn't told Lana the whole story of his struggle with his career. Someday he would. Even today, he wondered sometimes if the job suited him. He enjoyed the teens—cared about them with all his heart—but that was the problem. Would he be a good role model? Could he allow them to grow on their own terms without manipulating them?

He'd struggled against his parents' will for the sake of being an individual. Could he allow the students their individuality and still guide them in God's Word? The responsibility awed him, and he feared it. How much easier to be a coach. To list rules on sportsmanship and not be directing someone in God's rules. He didn't feel worthy. Maybe he should have forced his hand to register for the gym teacher and coach classes.

Why did he question God's will? Sometimes he wondered if God was forcing his will or if his own need to stay close to the Lord motivated him. Other times, he felt assured that God had led him for His own purposes. With his debut as a youth director at First Church of Holly, Mark prayed that the Lord would validate his decision.

Lana's image rose in his mind. He'd pushed her to the limit, but this too he sensed was God's direction. Since the day he'd watched her strut across her yard, wielding the hedge trimmer, he'd recognized a woman with spirit and a sense of humor. He loved both of those attributes. And despite her sometimes focusing on herself, he believed a compassionate heart beat within her. Obviously, Lana had embraced Jesus and was a true Christian—but a Christian, he feared, who had allowed one of her "fruits of the Spirit" to spoil on the vine. He grinned at his imaginative speculation, wondering how much of his own fruit was decaying.

He focused heavenward as a feeling of God's presence washed over him. The sunlight pierced through a billow of cumulus clouds like a heavenly beam striking the rippling water, almost as if God's spotlight stirred the lake and pinpointed the horizon. Could this camping experience be part of God's design? He'd already seen Lana change more than his teasing and pushing could have caused. And he felt his own heart moving closer to the Lord. Would being here bring Lana and him new insight into their relationship?

"Fancy meeting you here." Surprisingly good-natured, Lana's voice surged behind him.

A warm prickle rose on his neck, and he glanced at her over his shoulder.

"At least the camp manager apologized," she said, plopping down on the grass at his side. "He promised he'd make sure the bat found another cave to sleep in. . .since I can't." She tilted her head and shifted her body to view his face.

Mark touched her arm. "I'm sorry, Lana. The place isn't quite what the brochure said, but for our purpose, I pray it works. God's here as well as at the Ritz Hotel."

Lana covered his fingers with her own, her voice gentle. "To be honest, I prefer this to the Ritz." She shook her head and gazed around as if stunned. "I can't believe I said that."

"I hope you meant it, because I feel the same way." Her face shone in the warm sunlight, and his heart skipped, sensing their nearness.

"In some ways, I do. Though I admit a convenient bathroom would be awfully nice."

He agreed wholeheartedly, but he'd never utter the words or else he'd be rewarded with her I-told-you-so smile.

"Just be grateful," he said, knowing his comment had a cryptic element.

"Grateful for what?" She leaned forward and a scowl settled on her face.

"At least these flush."

Her chuckle rose on the quiet breeze. "I didn't think about that."

His attention turned toward the heavenly glow rippling on the lake. "We'll have our first Bible study after dinner tonight. When we're finished, I thought you could introduce the team activity you planned. If they're still not worn out when it's over, we'll end with a campfire and sing-along."

"That sounds safer than horseback riding." She turned her head slowly toward him. "I think." With her last comment, she rose.

"We could roast a few marshmallows," he said, as if that made it even safer.

She only grinned. "I'm heading back to check out the rest of the facilities. I need to know what else I'm in for."

❧

As Lana approached her cabin, the sound of youthful voices carried across the grass from the activity building, and in the open field, she saw a volleyball game in progress. The playful cheers and boos sailed to her ears and, for once, sounded inviting. Expecting the cabin to be empty, she faltered when she stepped inside. A dark-haired teen Lana didn't know raised her head from the pillow and looked at her, then lowered it again. The girl's eyes looked red rimmed, and Lana hesitated, wondering how the girl would react when she approached her.

"What's wrong?" she asked, then waited in silence for the teen to respond.

A muffled "I'm fine" rose from the sleeping bag.

Lana wandered to her own cot and sat, gazing at the girl two bunks over. "Doesn't sound like it."

"Doesn't really matter," the girl said.

Lana rose and slid onto the next bunk, facing her. "Sure it does." She waited a moment before she spoke again. "Sometimes having someone listen helps," Lana offered again.

"My parents say I have eternal PMS." Her voice muffled in her pillow.

Lana chuckled but couldn't help the pull of emotion as she looked at the bundle of sadness lying on the bunk. "It's good to have a sense of humor."

With apparent curiosity, the young woman lifted her head.

Lana smiled into her amazed, wide eyes. "I often laugh at myself. It's better than crying. . .and much better than getting angry."

The girl rolled on her side and propped her cheek against her fist. "I usually get angry. . .at myself. I rarely let other people know I'm upset. It doesn't do any good."

"What's the use of getting angry at yourself? Laughter's lots better." She moved closer to the teen. "For some reason, I haven't met you before. I'm Lana West."

The teenager paused, then nodded. "Janet. Janet Byrd. Or 'Bird the Nerd' as they call me." Her voice rang with sarcasm.

When she heard Janet's comment, Lana's stomach twisted with disappointment. So many times at the high school, she'd heard the taunting remarks of teens to one another. Sometimes they could be so cruel. But she expected Christians to behave better. "Do you mean one of the kids from church called you that?"

"No. I usually hear it at school." She stared at her pillow and then added, "My parents insisted that I come here. It wasn't my idea. Not at all."

Lana shifted and sat on the foot of Janet's bunk. "Ah, I can hear it now. 'Janet, it'll be good for you.'"

The girl sat up cross-legged, then grinned for the first time. "Right. I heard that when I was a little girl. 'Janet, this spanking hurts me more than it hurts you.'" She giggled.

"I remember hearing the same line. Do you think God programs that sentence into parents?"

"Could be," she said, taking a strand of hair and twirling it around her finger. "I guess I'm feeling sorry for myself. I've always been a loner. I don't come to the youth activities at church, so I don't know these kids."

"That makes it hard," Lana said, knowing now why she'd never met the girl.

"We moved to a rural area last year. I go to Fenton High, and most of the kids from church go to Holly or Davisburg."

"It's hard to get to know new people, isn't it? Especially if you're not involved in the activities. You attend church, though?"

She nodded. "But that's it. I don't drive yet, and my parents don't want to drop me off and pick me up for teen Sunday school and things, so. . ." Her voice faded away.

Lana gathered her thoughts. "Even though you don't know them well, Janet, you share something important with these kids."

"Not school." A look of frustration crossed her face.

"No, not school. Something much better and more important." The teen's expression shifted to curiosity.

"Jesus. That's much more important than everything. Give the kids a chance, Janet. I can't promise you miracles. You know as well as I do that teenagers can be great or they can be unkind, but hopefully, the kids at church camp will be an improvement over the high school students. The problem is you have to give a little too."

"They seem to look past me," she said, stretching her legs out and lowering her feet to the floor.

"It's because they don't know you, and when you look away or look uneasy, they protect their own feelings by not taking a chance to talk with you."

With a thoughtful look on her face, Janet shrugged.

Before Lana could pursue the subject any further, noise sounded outside the door. In a heartbeat, Susan and Teri bounded into the cabin and came to a screeching halt.

Teri looked from Lana to Janet. "Are you sick?" she asked Janet.

Janet gave Lana a nervous look, then turned her attention to the girls. "No. Just lazy."

"Lazy? That's better than being sick. I hate to be away from home and get sick." She plopped onto her bunk. "You should have been out with us. Then you'd really be nauseated."

Susan laughed. "Our volleyball score was terrible."

Teri eyed Janet from head to toe, then narrowed her eyes. "How tall are you?"

Janet looked at her long legs and stood. "Five-nine. Why?"

"Can you play volleyball?"

Janet nodded.

Teri turned to Susan and motioned to Janet. "The next game, huh?"

"For sure," Susan said.

Shifting her attention back, she folded her arms over her chest and looked at Janet. "Promise you'll be on our volleyball team tomorrow. Okay? We need someone tall like you."

With a sheepish grin, Janet looked at Lana before giving her answer. "Sure. Promise."

"Great," Teri said, crossing to her side and lopping her arm over Janet's shoulder. "Next time, we'll beat the pants off them."

nine

With Mark's help, Lana spent part of the afternoon trying to hide clues for the camp road rally without anyone seeing her. She'd dodged the campers numerous times, tucking eight clue packets into the haystack at the archery range, hiding another set in one of the canoes, hanging a plastic bag holding the next set in the shower, and putting the last ones in a coffee can behind an unoccupied cabin.

When the dinner bell sounded, Lana headed for the dining hall, praying for something tolerable. If the meals were as rustic as the setting, she'd beg Mark to find a small town nearby with a fast-food restaurant. As she stepped into the dining hall, the aroma of grease and hot dogs filled the room. What else should she have expected but frankfurters and French fries? While the fare may have pleased the teenagers, Lana hoped she'd brought along some antacid.

Mark signaled to her from across the room. She joined him and slid onto the bench at one of the long plank tables. When all the teens were accounted for, Mark rose. "Before we eat, who'd like to ask the blessing?"

No one spoke. "Okay, tonight I'll take a turn, but someone else can be ready tomorrow. Let's join hands."

Lana rose and was amazed as table after table of teens joined together until they had formed one big zigzag circle around the room.

Mark bowed his head, and his pleasant, resonant voice filled the room. "We thank You, Lord, for our safe journey here today, and we give thanks for the food prepared by our able chefs. We ask You to bless our two weeks together. Help us to learn to give up our own control over situations and trust solely in You. In Jesus' name we pray. Amen."

"And patience, Lord," Lana whispered, inserting her personal need into the prayer.

When the teens moved forward to fill their plates, cafeteria-style, chatter, and the clink of dishes filled the room. Lana sat and waited with Mark, unmotivated by the menu, yet hungry.

"Before you all go back for seconds," Mark said as a general announcement, "please let the camp counselors have some food too."

Laughter and taunting echoed around the room, and when the clamor faded, Lana rose and followed Mark to the food counter. After taking a healthy portion of salad, for which she was grateful, Lana accepted a hot dog and a portion of soggy fries. She decided to forgo dessert.

"Think you'll survive?" Mark whispered once they sat.

"Your guess is as good as mine," Lana answered, "but if I don't, bury me somewhere quiet. . .like in the woods." She sent him an eye-rolling grin.

"You're a good sport, Lana," he said, then opened his mouth and filled it with a bite of a hot dog and bun.

When the meal ended and the dishes were cleared from the table, Mark announced the Bible study. Lana watched Bibles appear from everywhere—back packs and shoulder bags. Some campers pulled small New Testaments from their back pockets.

"Since we're going to learn about teamwork and trust, let's look at one promise Jesus made," Mark said. "Open your Bibles to Luke 6:27."

Pages rustled and then silence.

Mark read the verses. " 'But I tell you who hear me: Love your enemies, do good to those who hate you, bless those who curse you, pray for those who mistreat you.' "

Lana heard the teens mumble among themselves, and

finally they turned toward Mark.

"So what does this have to do with us?" Mark asked.

Questions flew. How can we love our enemy? Does God really expect us to bless people who curse us? Though they'd heard the words before, the teens' disbelief resounded.

The discussion continued, and Lana watched Janet. She knew the girl had felt alone, and she'd wondered how the teen would handle this discussion topic.

"Jesus does this every day," Sara said.

"Huh?" Jason grunted.

"Jesus forgives us all the time for our sins and expects nothing in return," Sara responded. "If we're to follow Jesus, then we have to do the same, no matter how hard it is."

"That's right," Mark said. "Listen to this in verses 35 and 36: 'But love your enemies, do good to them, and lend to them without expecting to get anything back. Then your reward will be great, and you will be sons of the Most High, because he is kind to the ungrateful and wicked. Be merciful, just as your Father is merciful.' "

Lana let the meaningful discussion settle in her thoughts. She recalled the teens at her high school, wondering how many of them went to church and if they were eager to learn about Jesus like these teenagers seemed to be.

The vision, however, gave her hope. Maybe her attitude had been as much of a problem as her students themselves. Had she really given them an opportunity for input? Had she excited them in the same way Mark seemed to do about studying God's Word? Looking at her teaching in a new light sent a flutter of anticipation through her. Maybe next year things would be different.

"The important thing," Mark continued, "is to look for nothing. Don't expect a reward here on earth. Instead you'll find those treasures in heaven." He closed his Bible and ended with prayer.

"Campfire?" Gary asked from a front table.

"Later, maybe," Mark said. "First, we're going to have fun."

Groans filled the hall, and Lana couldn't hold back a smile.

"Lana's going to tell you about our camp version of a road rally. Remember our focus here is teamwork—cooperation, communication, and caring about others. Now it's time to break up into eight groups of four, and before you get too far away, make sure you all grab a flashlight. This rally may last until dark. "

Lana listened to the scraping of bench legs against the plank flooring as they rose. She watched in fear, praying that one teen wasn't left unselected and feeling unwanted, but in moments, she eyed the room and saw eight groups of four. Her focus first settled on Janet. Next she eyed Don, thrilled to see him among the campers. Both previously isolated teens stood with three others, looking animated and happy. Her heart lifted at the sight.

"Lana," Mark said, "tell them how this works."

Though an experienced teacher, Lana stood in front of the group feeling her own kind of apprehension. A classroom was her territory, not a camp meeting room, but she looked at the eager faces and began. After explaining the procedure, she watched enthusiasm grow in the room. "Does everyone understand before I give you the first puzzle?"

"What's the prize?" Susan asked.

"If we win, what do we get?" Jason echoed.

Mark laughed. "Now if you were listening to our Bible study, you wouldn't expect any reward on earth."

The room filled with laughter. Yet Mark had made a point.

"Let's not worry about the prize for now," he said. "The objective is to come in first with all of the puzzles solved."

The buzz of voices faded without an argument so Lana continued. "Select a team captain, and send your leader up for the first puzzle."

Following a chaotic moment, Lana distributed the clues, and the teams scattered, heading through the two screened doors to the outside.

"You did great," Mark said, sliding his arm around her waist. "What's the first clue?"

"You want to be on a team?" she asked, giving him a sly grin. "It's a bag of elbow macaroni with a note that says, 'Use your noodle.'"

"I know noodle means to use your head, but I'm sure it has another meaning. Right?" He grinned.

"Inside one of the elbows is a little note telling them where to go next."

"Not bad," he said. "Should we follow?"

She shook her head. "We'll probably get there before they will. But here's a question for you. What's the prize?"

"You're as bad as the kids," he said. "The camp administrator went into town, and I had him pick up a pizza. I'll pop it in the oven in an hour or so."

"Pizza?" Her stomach growled at the thought. "I love pizza."

"We don't always get the things we love," he said. "Not right away, anyway. Sometimes we have to wait."

His tender eyes sent her on a whirlpool journey to her heart. She sensed his words had a deeper meaning, and the reality fluttered through her like butterflies. Lifting her gaze to his, she couldn't speak.

Mark clasped her arm and guided her outside beneath the dusky sky. "Let's go check out the fire pit. I'm sure they'll want a campfire before bed."

She walked beside him, and he wove his fingers through hers as they made their way toward the sandy fire ring. The scent of pines and earth sailed on the air, and Lana inhaled the aroma, feeling that God had given her a reprieve from everyday experiences—even though she had fought the opportunity.

She fought so many things. The concept weighed on her mind. Would she ever give up the fight and let God take control?

She looked up at Mark, admiring his strong profile against the setting sun. Could Mark be part of God's plan? They'd known each other such a short time. Maybe two months. Yet Lana felt close to him and comfortable. Her heart fluttered at the touch of his hand, and her pulse skipped like a child at recess when he gazed into her eyes.

"Why so quiet?" Mark asked.

"The quiet sounds nice, doesn't it?"

"You're thoughtful." He squeezed her fingers. "Sorry you came?"

"Never. I'm learning more than the kids are."

He gave her a surprised look. "What do you mean?"

"About my teaching style. . .and my attitude. I know I have a long way to go, but maybe it wasn't you who motivated me to come here. Do you think it might have been God?"

His smile brightened the shadowy surroundings. "God works in mysterious ways."

She nodded, enjoying the conversation and the feel of Mark's arm brushing against hers.

Close to the lake, they found the fire pit. Fallen logs formed a wide circle around a sandy hollow piled with kindling and fire wood. A generous supply of split wood stood nearby.

"Looks good," she said.

He nodded, then slipped his fingers from hers and guided his arm around her waist. Turning toward the lake, Lana stepped along with Mark, and when they reached the narrow strip of sand, he paused.

"Nothing like a sunset on the water," he said. "When I see beauty like this, I wonder how anyone can doubt God controlling the order of things. Such systematic detail can't happen by chance."

Lana looked across the multicolored lake, rippling with

orange, gold, and coral splotches. "I think people are afraid to believe because they think they'll lose their free will like God will take over their lives. They don't understand. Even with God, we make choices and decide the path we follow. Trouble is, some of us make bad choices and follow misleading paths." She released a disheartened chuckle, knowing she'd made many bad decisions in her life.

"Do you have someone specific in mind?" Mark asked, his voice teasing.

"Not a soul," she said, understanding he knew better.

He glanced at his watch and turned away from the lake. "I'd better get that pizza in the oven or our winning team will have a cold prize."

When they returned to the activity hall, it stood empty. Mark headed for the kitchen, and Lana checked her clue list, guessing how far the teens had gotten in their solutions. She'd left the canoes for last, and since no one was at the lake when she and Mark were there, she figured it would be awhile longer before the winners arrived.

To her surprise, only fifteen minutes passed before the winning team came through the door, bursting with conversation and laughter. "Did we win?" Janet asked, scanning the empty room.

"You sure did," Lana said. "Congratulations."

The girls let out a squeal, and Mark came to the kitchen doorway. "Your prize is almost ready."

Sniffing like bloodhounds, the four girls hurried toward the kitchen while giggles and noise sailed through the doorway.

Lana heard the screen door open and turned, watching another group file inside. Seeing the empty room, their faces broke into grins, then faded when they saw the girls coming from the kitchen with the pizza.

Despite their disappointment, conversation rolled with stories of how they'd followed the clues and where they'd made mistakes. As each team arrived, they watched the girls scarfing down the pungent pizza, and soon they wanted no more watching.

"How about a campfire?" Gary said. "At least we can eat marshmallows."

At the word campfire, conversation hummed. Mark gave the go-ahead, and the door swung open and slammed closed as they darted outside. Voices raised with comments about finding a stick to whittle and heading back to their bunks for their stash of marshmallows.

"Ready?" Mark asked. "The girls can finish that pizza alone." He gave them a wink.

"Save us a seat," Teri called.

Mark nodded and turned to Lana. "We'll get our flashlights and head down."

Without hesitation, Lana agreed. The scent of the tangy pizza had stirred her appetite, and she had considered mugging the girls for one little piece.

Mark clasped her elbow as they stepped outside, and as always, Lana liked the cozy feeling. She sensed his enthusiasm for the whole day, and she admired his Christian love for his work, his youthful charges, and the Lord. Mark seemed the epitome of trust. Lana had no question that she loved God, but she prayed the rest of Mark's qualities would rub off on her even a little.

Clutching flashlights, she and Mark headed for the wooded clearing. When the fire blazed, everyone scooted forward with anticipation, awaiting the perfect moment to toast their marshmallows over the glowing coals.

One of the boys brought along a guitar and strummed some familiar campfire tunes. Little by little, voices joined in singing.

Mark sat beside Lana with a jackknife, whittling pointed ends on long sticks for the marshmallows, and as he passed them out, the marshmallow bags were opened, and the white puffs of sweetness were skewered to the ends.

Lana marveled at the blackened, flaming globs they pulled off the stick ends and ate. She sat near the fire and, with great patience, rotated her stick, holding it the proper distance for the golden brown version she preferred.

"Here, Lana," one of the boys said, thrusting a coal black ash in front of her. "See it's perfect. You can have it."

"Thanks, Bernie," she said, "I'm doing fine."

Bernie eyed her with curiosity while she continued to rotate the spear, admiring the golden, swelling puff. Perfection. "There," she said, "now this is what I call a toasted marshmallow."

As she pulled the stick forward, the soft confection lost its housing and dropped into the fire and burst into flame.

"That's what I call garbage," Jason chortled.

"How about making me one just like that," Gary joked. The group nearby tittered as they watched her golden masterpiece burning in the fire pit.

Purpose rose in her, and she thrust another one onto the end and again pivoted the stick slowly at the perfect height from the coals, watching the deepening bronze. With great pride, she pulled the marshmallow forward—more carefully this time—but a passing teen bumped her stick, and her prize marshmallow fell to the ground. She scowled at the teen and snatched another white orb from the bag.

Mark laughed. "Is it really that important?"

"Yes," she muttered. "I'm demonstrating the art of toasting a proper marshmallow."

"Look," one of the boys called and waved his stick toward Lana to show off his near perfect exhibit. But the loose, gooey mass flew from his skewer, and the confection sailed through the air and tangled in Lana's hair. A gasp rippled around the circle.

The young man gaped at the empty point on his stick, then at the others around him. "Hey! Who snatched my marshmallow?"

While the teens tittered at his distrust, Lana pulled away the gooey lump now decorated with strands of her brown locks. "Here you go," she said, extending the mess toward him.

His eyes widened. "Wow! I'm sorry, Lana. But do you see how perfect it is?"

"Was," someone called out.

The crowd laughed him into embarrassment, and Lana gazed at the sticky goo. "Sure thing. That's what I call perfect."

With the mess smeared on her fingers, she rose. "I guess I'd better beat the girls to the shower so I get dibs on the hot water." She leaned toward Mark and sent her most satirical voice his way. "I'm glad the ladies have the night shift." She sent him a sweet wave and pattered down the path toward the cabin.

Though she'd joked, Lana winced at her behavior. *It's my way or no way. Like Mark said, did it really make that much difference about the marshmallow?* She'd begun toasting it for fun—as a challenge to herself and to demonstrate what a really great glob of golden perfection looked like. Instead, she'd frowned and behaved like an idiot. Mark deserved so much more than a woman with her pitiful amount of self-control.

After the shower when she crawled into her sleeping bag, Lana relived her last disillusionment of the day. Needing a schedule to share the same shower stalls seemed bad enough, but no one had prepared her for the other news.

Ice cold water.

ten

Mark relaxed. Two days had passed without incident. *Serious incident,* he corrected, thinking of the bandages, bruises, and narrow escape when two teens at the archery range decided to play William Tell.

He savored the time with Lana. Though he still caught her familiar grimace on occasion—like the night of the first bonfire—she'd grown, and so had he. He no longer struggled for courage to slip his arm around her shoulders or grasp her hand as they walked. Those actions had become natural. But he'd not kissed her, and the desire banged around in his head like the cabin bats and made his pulse pick up its pace.

Should he? The question soared through his mind. If he kissed her, would things change? If Lana resisted, would it build a barrier between them? They'd known each other such a short time in contrast to the age-old feelings that wove through his heart. Mark felt certain he loved her. Not for her pretty face and shapely figure—and definitely not for her stubbornness—but for her wit, her intelligence, and her humanity. Though she fought it, her compassion had blossomed like a spring flower.

But Mark felt uncertain. How could he know for sure how Lana felt about him? At first, he figured she found him amusing. Maybe a challenge. But lately, she accepted his friendship without question and didn't pull away when his arm wrapped around her. He suspected she enjoyed it. He even noted a softer, more intimate whisper when she spoke, avoiding the ears of the teens that surrounded them most of the time. But was his interpretation correct or only wishful thinking?

Feeling upbeat, he roused himself early on the third day of

camp with a happy heart. Today he'd planned another team activity. The first had been successful, and he hoped while they had fun and a sense of competition among the teams, they were learning those attributes he'd discussed with them.

With a light heart, he stepped outside and confronted the director heading toward him. The director's desperate expression slowed Mark's upbeat spirit to a dirge.

"Sorry," he said. "This is bad news. The cook and her assistant have both come down with the flu. The twenty-four-hour kind, they've both assured me, but. . ."

Mark heard his lengthy hesitation, and his heart sank. "But?"

"I haven't found anyone able to prepare the day's meals. I even asked my wife, but she has a commitment she can't break. The cook said if she can drag herself here later for dinner she would, but we still have breakfast and lunch to worry about."

"So what should we do?" Mark asked, hoping the man had some ideas.

"We have some cold cereal, I think. Maybe we could look together," the man said.

Mark's culinary interests slipped into first gear. All he needed was a helper. "Let me see what I can do."

The director nodded, his expression grateful.

Mark's mind whirred in thought. Breakfast he could handle. Sandwiches would get them through lunch, and he prayed by evening the cook would recover enough to scrounge up a feeble dinner. He stood for a heartbeat gazing heavenward. *Lord, I need a little guidance here.*

His body involuntarily shifted, facing Lana's quiet cabin. He glanced into the clouds again, closed his eyes for moral support, and forged across the grass. She slept near the window, and he rapped gently on the shuttered glass and pressed his lips close to the pane. "Lana." He rapped again and waited.

No sound came from inside. His knuckle plinked the glass

again. "Lana, I need to talk with you."

A slight rustle moved behind the shutter. He waited. A weary face peered from the narrow space between the door and frame. "What?" she whispered. "I have eight sleeping girls in here. What's wrong?"

Her expression changed when she opened the door a hairbreadth wider. "You look like someone stole your bicycle. What is it?"

The words tumbled from his mouth, and he watched her shoulders tighten beneath her sweatshirt, then droop like a receding tide.

She shook her head. "I suppose I'm in this thing for the duration." A rattled sigh escaped her. "Give me a few minutes. I'll meet you in the kitchen."

His own relieved sigh rippled through his chest, and with a confident wave, he darted across the dewy grass to the back door of the dining hall. The building was lighted, and the camp director, his mouth agape, stood between the large work counter and huge iron stove, pivoting in a slow circle like a weather vane caught in a strange wind. "I don't even know where to begin," he groaned.

"Leave," Mark said. "I'll take over breakfast, but I expect a generous refund on this venture." He stood his ground until the man nodded.

"I suppose it's worth it," the director said and hustled through the doorway like a man newly paroled.

Mark stared into the refrigerator. What would be quick and easy? Cereal, he thought, but today was their big canoe day. The teens needed energy. Scrambled eggs? With cheese? Fast and easy. Add toast, and he had his breakfast menu.

By the time he'd hauled out the ingredients, a blurry-eyed Lana stalked through the door.

"Okay, Betty, what can I do?"

"Who?" He squinted at her, trying to decode her thinking.

"Crocker. Betty Crocker," she enunciated. "What can I do, Chief?"

He laughed. "That's chef. Isn't it?"

"We'll see about that, won't we?" She gave his arm a poke and stepped up to the food-laden counter. They worked side by side, cracking dozens of eggs and beating them into a foamy mass. Then he grated cheese while she buttered bread.

When she slipped the big crock of butter back into the refrigerator, she stood, staring inside. "We ought to do something interesting. Give the eggs a little zip."

"Zip? What are you talking about? Kids don't like zip. They like plain, regular stuff. Things they know."

She didn't move. "I've heard of adding mayonnaise to eggs."

"Forget it, Lana. Let's stick with cheese."

Before he could stop her, she swung around and unleashed the cap from a bottle. "Here we go. Just a dash for added flavor."

He attempted to shift the mixing bowl, but the bathtub-sized container made shifting more challenging. She caught the edge with her zip before Mark could read the label. An enormous splash appeared, and the eggs swam with a dark red liquid.

She pulled back, staring at the bottle. "Oops." She eyed the label, her face paling.

Mark froze like a Thanksgiving turkey. "What do you mean, oops?"

"I thought it was a shaker bottle." She hid the label behind her back like a little kid caught in the cookie jar. "I meant to grab the Worcestershire Sauce."

"So what is it? What did you put in the eggs?"

She swung the bottle around to face him. "Hot sauce."

He cringed. "Hot sauce. Wonderful."

She shrugged sheepishly. "Okay. . .so what do we do now?"

"We?" He narrowed his eyes and allowed a scowl to settle

on his face. "I'm going to announce you threw hot sauce in the eggs."

"Come on, Mark. Think. We can call them Mexicali eggs. Teens like tacos and things."

Biting her lower lip, Lana scanned the room with a look of desperation until she lurched forward and snatched up a half-empty bag of corn chips. She squeezed the bag, and the crunch and crackle sounded through the room.

Panic rifled through Mark's mind, but again, his body reacted more slowly than Lana's. She pulled open the bag and dumped the crumbled chips into the eggs.

"What are you doing?" Mark asked, his imagination flying.

Grabbing the whisk, she swirled the hot sauce and chips through the eggs. *"Voila!"*

"That's French. How about *'Vaya con Dios'?"* He felt his shoulders sag and his spirits with them.

"Don't be a bad sport." She spun toward him, looking like a mountain climber reaching the top of Everest. "It may be delicious."

"May is the operative word." He leaned against the counter for support. If she ruined breakfast, what would he do?

Lana turned her back on him and tore through the cabinets looking for the proper-sized pans and griddles. Gigantic seemed to be the smallest. He took two huge frying pans from her and divided the mixture, pouring half into each.

Lana had grown quiet. She covered two burners with a wide griddle and tossed the buttered bread on top.

When the clock hands reached seven-thirty, Lana rang the breakfast bell and returned with speed to set out the jugs of milk and the pots of water for hot chocolate. The first comer burst threw the doorway and came to a screeching halt.

The boy's eyes opened nearly as wide as the plates sitting in a pile on the serving table. "What are you two doing here?"

Mark chuckled at the teen's expression. "I've always wanted

to be a cook. Let me know if I should change careers." *But not with this meal,* he thought, wondering how the boy would react when he tasted Lana's concoction.

"I'm an innocent bystander," Lana added.

Mark sent her one of his sternest looks but made no comment.

The parents and teens piled into the hall, and after Gary said the blessing, the huge mound of cheesy eggs and grilled toast nearly vanished. To Mark's amazement, the breakfast received rave reviews. Lana pranced in the kitchen like she'd won a blue ribbon at a bake-off.

Before the campers scraped the bottom of the serving dish, Mark put a couple of spoonfuls on a plate and eyed the scrambled mess. He dipped his fork into the mixture and slid a bite into his mouth. He grinned and took two more tastes. The creamy cheese sauce blended with the hot sauce and chips, leaving a spirited flavor in his mouth. Lana had been right. The Mexicali creation tasted like real Mexican cuisine.

Disappointment slithered over faces when they came back for more and found an empty bowl. When the scraping forks quieted, Mark slipped out of his discolored apron and joined his charges in the dining room. "We'll have our Bible study this morning since today is our canoe trip and tonight we have another team activity."

Cheers and voices rose above his, and he quieted them before continuing. "Hold on, pals. When we're finished with our lesson, we'll meet at the hut by the beach. Pair off before you get there. We'll be heading for a park a few miles downstream. When we arrive, we'll have a picnic, and the bus will bring us back. The camp director will take care of the canoes."

"You mean we don't get to canoe back?" Sara asked.

"No," Mark said

Moans and groans hummed around the hall.

Mark shook his head, realizing they knew little about canoeing. "You'll thank me. Did you ever try to canoe upstream?"

From the teens' expression, Mark knew they had no idea about upstream or downstream, and he realized a quick canoeing lesson would be a must before they paddled away later in the morning.

"Open your Bibles," Mark said, "to Romans 15:13–14. Look over the verses. I'll be right back." He hurried to the kitchen, realizing he had to break the bad news to Lana.

"We have a problem. . .as you know," he said, eyeing her in dishwater up to her elbows. "I have to lead the Bible study so I'll see if the other counselors will come in and help you. Okay?"

"What if I say no?" Her arms hung at her sides, and water dripped onto the plank floor.

"It's only two jobs. Finish the dishes, and make sandwiches for the canoe trip. And you can bring along some of those apples too," he said gesturing toward the peck of fruit on a counter. He ducked as a soggy dishcloth flew through the air, missing him by a soap bubble. He gave her his sweetest smile and escaped back into the dining room.

The parents cooperated, and with the magnified sounds of dishes being washed and put away along with a few door-bangs and muffled groans coming from the kitchen, Mark began the lesson.

He opened his Bible and faced the group. "You've had a chance to read these two verses. What do you think Paul means, and what does the message have to do with us? Listen again: 'May the God of hope fill you with all joy and peace as you trust in Him, so that you may overflow with hope by the power of the Holy Spirit. I myself am convinced, my brothers, that you yourselves are full of goodness, complete in knowledge and competent to instruct one another.' "

The discussion got underway, and Mark prodded and

encouraged their understanding of hope and trust in each other as well as in God. "When you get in the canoes a short time from now, some of you might be experienced and some not. These verses remind us to listen to your partner's knowledge and learn from his or her instructions. Don't think you know better. Remember, we are all full of goodness—which means cooperation and concern for each other."

With his final words, Mark sent the teens and parent counselors on their way to dress for the canoe trip, then bolstered his courage to face Lana. When he slid into the kitchen, she was alone. He watched her for a moment before she noticed him. "Hi, Camperella. Where are your helpers?" he asked.

Perspiration glistened on her nose, and mustard decorated her fingers. "Camperella?" She gave him a quizzical look. "Oh, I get it," she said, with a slight smirk. "They went to the ball without me." She stuck her foot toward him. "Where's my glass slipper, Prince Uncharming?"

He looked at her tiny feet clad in damp, food-stained sneakers. Seeing her at work—work she'd agreed to do to bail him out—touched him. He sidled next to her, sliding his arm around her waist. She turned her shiny face upward, and he grabbed a paper towel to daub the moist droplets sitting on her nose. "My poor friend, I've worked you way too hard."

"It's hot when you're up to your elbows in dishwater."

"I know." A strong urge soared through him to kiss her upturned lips. Like a magnet, the attraction drew him forward, and without thinking, his mouth met hers in a sweep of tenderness. To his joy, she didn't pull away, but tiptoed upward and returned the touch with such gentleness it might have been a dream. But he knew better, and so did his heart, hammering like a woodpecker.

When he eased away, Lana lifted her eyes to his with a look of surprise. But her expression shifted to acceptance, then pleasure. His joy soared, and he longed to return to her sweet mouth, but caution waved a flag in his thoughts. He'd wait for another time and another place.

With a hint of embarrassment, she lowered her eyes. "Everything's ready," she said. "The sandwiches and sodas are packed in the two coolers. I put the apples in this box." She gestured to a carton sitting beside the coolers. "Then we'd better get ready too," Mark said, wishing he could do something wonderful for her kindness.

They closed the kitchen, and as they headed out the back door, the director flagged Mark.

"The cook is still sick, but I have good news," he said. "I found a replacement for dinner tonight."

Mark stepped toward him. "That's a relief." He motioned toward the kitchen. "The coolers and box of apples are ready to go."

"Good work," the man said. "The bus should be there long before your group arrives."

"I hope so," Mark said, beginning to wonder if any more catastrophes might occur.

Outside, Mark and Lana headed in the direction of their cabins to slip into clothing suitable for the canoe trip. Both ready, they crossed the lawn together and headed to the lake. When they arrived, most of the teens were waiting and immediately started egging him to get going. The canoes had been lined up on the shore, and Mark glanced at the map and instructions, praying for a safe outing.

While Mark checked to see who still seemed to be missing, Lana motioned each pair together and assigned them a canoe. She surprised him when she moved to his side and whispered. "Problem, I think."

"What?" he asked.

She gave him a subtle tilt of her head.

He surveyed the groups of twosomes and spotted the problem. "Janet?" he whispered back.

Lana nodded. "She's been great since that first day. She and Teri hit it off, but I think Teri's paired up with Dennis."

Mark eyed the boy and girl, standing together. "What happened to Susan? Weren't they all friends?"

"She's not feeling well and asked one of the parents if she could stay in the cabin."

Mark eyed the situation. "So what do you think we should do now?"

"You'll canoe alone, and I'll tell Janet I don't have a partner."

"Or we could include her in the rowboat with the two fellows."

Lana's raised eyebrow told him that wasn't the answer. He unwillingly conceded. "Okay, but I thought you've never canoed before."

She gave him one of her how-dumb-do-you-think-I-am looks. "It can't be that hard to learn," she said, one hand on her hip.

"It's tricky, Lana. You have to be—" He was talking to himself. Lana had bounded away and returned dragging Janet, wearing a smile on her lips.

Janet's face seemed a mixture of relief and embarrassment, but Lana rattled on as if the choice were hers, not caused by Janet's obvious exclusion from the other pairings.

Mark's caution about canoeing had fallen on Lana's deaf ears. Knowing Lana, she would do as she pleased. He decided to let it go and gathered the others for a review of canoeing instructions. "Now when you climb in, step to the center, and do it carefully." Fearing the worst, his eyes sought heaven.

"And remember," he continued, "follow each other, and don't try to play hero. Remember, we have the rowboat handy for emergencies." He paused whispering up another plea. "And no silliness. When we reach the park, pull over to the shore. You'll recognize it by picnic tables and a big bus."

They all laughed, and when he finished, the teams clambered into the canoes, some nearly toppling at the shoreline.

Within minutes, the caravan of canoes floated out to the center of the lake. Mark signaled for them to take the sharp turn into the narrower branch of the river where they would be pulled downstream toward a larger lake.

The rowboat stayed behind, keeping an eye out for toppled canoes, and Mark, navigating alone, lingered midway, watching the progress of the eager teens. His heart sank when he viewed Lana and Janet zigzagging their way far behind most of the canoes. Janet appeared to know a little about canoeing, but his instinct suggested that Lana was doing her thing. The teen didn't have a chance.

Despite her stubbornness, he was proud of Lana. Though her attitude about teens seemed to have been tarnished by her teaching position, she had given it another try and had succeeded. He admired the way she'd worked with the campers. He'd been touched by her sensitivity to Janet and her earlier response to Don. Lana might think she didn't like teens and teaching, but she seemed a different woman since they'd arrived at camp.

The rowboat passed him by and, concerned about Lana, Mark slowed and looked over his shoulder. Instead of continuing, he held back until her canoe drew closer. "How are you doing?" he called.

She gave him an exaggerated thumbs-up, but from the look on Janet's face, Mark guessed they weren't doing as well as Lana's thumb indicated.

When they came closer, Janet gave him a pitiful look. "She's worse than a teenager, Mark. She won't listen to a thing." Janet grinned, but the girl had pinpointed reality. Lana had grown so much, but at times, she slid into her old ways and needed to be in charge.

Mark viewed Janet's paddling skills and noticed Lana would have been better in the back, working as the rudder. Maybe because of her petite size, her oars hit the water with uneven strokes. Janet's long arms and taller stature could shoot them through the water while Lana's dragging paddles seemed to slow them down. Before Mark could stop himself, he'd uttered his thoughts aloud.

"Then we'll trade spots," Lana said, standing in the canoe and shifting her weight toward the back.

Mark let out a cautionary yell while Janet grabbed the canoe's sides and struggled to keep it upright. But in Lana's case, the struggle failed, and she tumbled from the canoe along with the paddle. When she resurfaced, Lana and the paddle had parted company.

Mark fought to turn his canoe back, but the current pulled him forward. He saw no way for Lana to climb back into either canoe without tipping them over. If he dived in to help her, he'd lose his own canoe. The logical course seemed for him to charge ahead for the rowboat.

"Swim to the side, Lana," he called, "and I'll get the rowboat to pick you up." He dug his paddle deep into the water, moving the canoe downstream. As he flew forward, Lana's paddle bobbed up and floated past. Leaning over with caution, he grabbed it before the paddle vanished into the debris along the riverbank.

Mark plunged his paddle from side to side at a racer's pace until he sighted the rowboat ahead of him. Yelling and waving to capture their attention, Mark moved forward, but his mind backed up, returning to the rubble swirling along the river's edge. He prayed a water snake hadn't chosen Lana's bank to sunbathe.

Finally, the teens in the rowboat spotted him and turned around. He thanked the Lord he'd had the forethought to prepare for an emergency. The boys gave Mark an acknowledging wave, reversed course, and sailed past on the way to Lana's rescue.

Mark back-paddled, waiting and praying Lana didn't panic.

Janet came by with panic etched on her face. "I'm sorry," she called as the current pulled her past. "If I'd realized what she was doing, I'd have—"

"Not your fault, Janet. You can't stop a freight train."

She nodded knowingly and skimmed by on her way to join the others.

Holding his position, Mark stroked backward as the current pulled him forward. Finally, he heard the rowboat's splash behind him, and Mark turned to spot a wet and scowling Lana, her hair straggling over her forehead like seaweed.

"Nice job," he teased, hoping he'd get a smile.

"I was waist-deep in frogs," she called. "Great big ugly things."

"Could have been worse," he said, following alongside the rowboat.

"Worse? Explain that to me." Her arms flailed in a wild gesture.

Though he tried to control his amusement, Mark grinned, seeing her dripping and madder than—he chuckled at his appropriate imagery—a wet hen. "Better than snakes."

Panic covered her face.

"You could have landed in a nest of water snakes."

"You mean to tell me there are snakes here?" She clung to the wooden side and stared into the dark, rolling water. For a heartbeat, she lifted her gaze toward Mark, then returned her attention to the water. "You aren't kidding, are you?"

His voice reverberated into the trees. "Come on, Lana. Would I kid you?"

As his canoe skimmed past her, Lana scowled darkly.

eleven

Lana pulled her legs underneath the rowboat bench and glowered. She felt utterly humiliated. Of all the boaters, she had been the only one to fall into the river. . .and only one of the two adults who had ventured out in the canoes.

As the boat brought her closer to shore, the teens stood around their canoes moored in the sand and gaped at her. Her clothes clung to her like plaster, and her wet hair sagged around her face.

When the rowboat beached, Janet ran toward her, her face filled with apology, and Lana felt swamped by guilt. She had caused her own spill, not the teenager. Hoping to calm the girl, Lana pushed a grin onto her face.

Without seeming concerned about getting wet, Janet threw her arms around Lana's neck. "I'm so sorry. I tried to stop you, but it was too late."

"Janet, it wasn't your fault. I did it to myself." She patted the girl's arm to calm her.

"I know but—"

"But nothing. You'd have fallen over yourself if you'd done anything else." Lana stepped back from the girl, now nearly as wet as she was. "Thanks for trying to stop me. I'm not what you'd call a sailor."

Mark slid next to them. "That's a little fishy." He grinned.

Lana lifted an eyebrow, acknowledging his corny joke.

"Now, now, don't be a wet blanket," he said.

Both eyebrows flew up while the campers grinned at their interaction.

Mark rested his arm against her damp shoulder. "Better yet,

we've all heard of the Frog Prince. We could crown you the Frog Princess?"

Lana took a playful poke at his arm. "Watch out, or I'll turn you into a wart."

The teens cheered at her comment. Lana thrust her nose into the air and turned on her heel as she snagged Janet by the arm. "We're not appreciated here, Janet. Let's find better company."

Janet grinned as they headed toward the picnic table where the hungriest campers were unloading the coolers.

A small group of teens gathered around Janet, and Lana couldn't avoid hearing their conversation.

"Great save," Teri said.

"You really know how to keep your canoe from flipping," Don added.

Sara poked Jason in the side. "Next time, I vote for Janet in my canoe. You nearly flipped us twice."

"I did not," Jason said, looking indignant.

Don shifted forward and moved to Janet's side. "Next time, Janet can be in my canoe. . .if you'd like," he said to her. A faint tinge of nervousness slid up his neck, but he stood his ground.

"Sure," Janet said, her own flush rising to her cheeks. Her gaze fastened to Lana's as happiness settled on her face.

"Let's eat," someone called.

Lana smiled, watching Janet being pulled along by the chattering teens, and she was touched by Don's interest in the girl. She raised her eyes heavenward and sent up a prayer of thanks. Looking toward the picnic table, Lana noticed that Janet had melted into the crowd. She herself longed to melt into the earth in her sodden, river-smelling garb.

She waited until the crowd had settled on the grass with their fruit and sandwiches until she wandered to an empty picnic table to slip off her waterlogged sneakers and socks. The air felt warmer on her water-soaked feet. Leaning her elbow on the plank tabletop, Lana rested her cheek against her fist, scrutinizing the noisy, fun-loving teens. Though hungry, her appetite had been squelched by the frogs.

The days she'd spent at camp skittered through her thoughts like mice in a cheese factory. Mark's kiss lingered in her mind, the tender warmth that left her heart jogging. Other memories were not so pleasant, like her marshmallow drama or the spill in the river. But through it all, she'd learned a lesson. When things went wrong, she seemed to be at the helm. Breakfast could have been a disaster—God had graciously gotten her out of that one—and her fall from the canoe could have left her or someone else injured.

Why did she always have to take over? She needed to work on that. Even more, she needed to pray about it instead of tackling it alone.

Lana looked around for Mark and saw him near the rowboat. She felt alone and wondered why he hadn't come to talk with her. She feared he was angry with her foolishness.

With that concern still in her thoughts, she heard Mark's voice. Did he call her name? She glanced around to see what he wanted. He stood away from the others, holding a dark green plastic bag and beckoned to her. She rose and walked to him, dragging her bare feet through the grass.

"Hey, Pal," he said, brushing her damp hair away from her cheeks. "How would you like some dry clothes?"

She looked at him, wondering what he meant. "Where would I get dry clothes?"

He held out the plastic bundle. "I came prepared."

She opened the bag and peeked inside. "What's this?" She fingered the garments. "Your clothes?"

"Just a pair of jogging shorts and a T-shirt. The shorts have a drawstring. I threw them in at the last minute—just in case."

"You figured I'd do something stupid. Right?"

"It could have been anyone. I thought you'd prefer to be dry."

She accepted his explanation and was touched by his thoughtfulness. "That was nice of you. Thanks."

Lana looked around, wondering where to change, and spotted a wooded area nearby. She flagged Janet.

When the girl arrived, Lana showed her the plastic bag. "How about standing guard while I change?"

Janet's face brightened. "I've been wishing I could do something since you fell in. This is easy."

She followed Lana toward the wooded area, and while Lana hid behind a tree, sliding out of her clothes and into Mark's, Janet watched for intruders.

"I'll be dressed in a minute," Lana said, dragging the clinging, wet clothes from her body.

"I don't mind," Janet said. "I've wanted to talk with you alone anyway. This gives me a chance."

"Oh?" Lana said, curious what the girl had to say.

"I wanted to thank you for talking to me when we first got here. You don't know how much it meant to me," Janet said.

Lana stopped a moment, wanting to run over and hug the girl, but her state of undress held her back. "It wasn't me, Janet. When the girls came in and saw you upset, their concern let you know they cared. And that changed you. I'm thrilled it happened."

"The best part is I feel better. I'm not afraid to be who I am. . . even at school. I know it'll still hurt me when kids act bogus, but I'll know I have friends at church and, best of all, I know I have a friend in Jesus. . .like you said."

"What you just said couldn't make me happier." Lana thought about Don and wondered if she should bring up the subject.

"And then Don's been so nice," Janet added

Lana's smile blossomed behind the girl's back. "I wanted to say something about that but hesitated. He's a nice boy. And sensitive."

"I know. He's told me about his family. It's great to have someone to talk to. Wait until I get home and tell my parents how glad I am I came here."

Dropping her soggy clothes into the plastic bag, Lana stepped from behind the tree and slid her arm around the girl's shoulder. "Isn't God awesome?"

"He sure is," Janet said.

With private grins, they headed back to the others.

Lana returned to the picnic table, and after she gathered up her shoes, Mark arrived with two sodas in one hand, three sandwiches in the other, and apples bulging from his pockets. "You feel okay?"

She saw no silly grin on his face for once, only his tender gaze. "I'm drier now. Other than that, my ego's a little injured, but I'm fine."

"Here." He offered her a sandwich, then set everything else on the table. "I'll say a blessing before we eat."

Earlier Lana had watched others around the park doing the same, bowing their heads in prayer with their hands joined. She liked the custom. She'd never prayed that way before the camping trip, and the act filled her with a sense of Christian fellowship. Maybe that's what she'd never experienced—a true sense of the communion of saints.

Mark slid onto the bench and took her hands in his. They bowed their heads, and Mark quietly prayed, giving thanks for the food and the day. Before he ended, he added a postscript. "Oh, and Lord, thank you for Lana's safety. And Father, could You help this woman learn that You are the captain of the ship? Teach her to trust in others and in You."

Saying amen, he squeezed her fingers, then grabbed a sandwich from the table and tore off the wrapper. "I'm starving." He bit into the bread, then paused and peered at her. "Not hungry?"

"Thinking, I guess." With an effort, she pulled herself from her thoughts. She took time unwrapping the waxed paper she'd folded so carefully around the bread and meat earlier that day.

"Thinking what?" Mark asked.

"What you said about teaching me to trust others, because the same idea sailed into my mind a few minutes ago."

"Lana, you're a sweet lady—"

"But with a few minor flaws," she said, tucking her damp hair behind her ear.

"But only a few," he said. "And very minor."

❧

Exhausted, Lana stood in her cabin, pleased the one-shower schedule gave the women's cabins priority to use the facility in the evening. On the ride back from the canoe trip, her frazzled thoughts had focused on taking a shower. She slipped off Mark's damp clothes, wrapped herself in her robe, and darted the few yards to the shower building. Even the cold water running over her tired body felt good, and when she dried and dressed in clean clothes, she felt human again.

Outside, the campers gathered on the grass, waiting for the dinner bell and reliving the events of their afternoon canoe trip. Lana noticed Janet sitting with Don and enjoyed being a witness to their blossoming relationship. The excitement on the river had made Janet more popular among the group, and little by little, she was coming out of her shell.

Mark joined Lana, smelling of herbal soap and wearing clean clothes. Though he'd been deprived shower privileges, she knew he'd done his best to freshen up.

"You look good," he said, sinking onto the grass beside her.

"I feel better. And look," she said, nodding slightly toward Janet.

"A budding romance. That's nice."

"They're two people who need each other," Lana added.

Mark's fingers slid over hers resting in the grass. "I know

two other people in the same boat."

"You mean canoe," she said, making a joke to hide her pleasure.

"Now who's the one joking about something serious?" He squeezed her hand.

The dinner bell rang, saving her from admitting he was right, and Mark rose and helped her from the ground. They joined the campers heading inside and took their seats in the dining hall. A wonderful aroma drifted from the kitchen.

"I wonder if it really smells that good or if I'm starving?" Lana asked

"Both, I think." He leaned over close to her ear. "But you smell best. Fresh, soapy, and wonderful."

"Probably because I reeked earlier."

"Never," he said, brushing his finger over her skin.

The sensation filled her with simple pleasure. Never had she had such a sense of partnership and sharing.

When almost everyone had arrived, Mark stood and surveyed the group of upturned faces. "Thank you for the safe and fun day. I'm proud of all of you. You followed the rules, and we're all back in one piece."

Lana heard a few titters and knew they were aimed at her.

Mark glanced down at her, and the laughter rose a couple decibels. "I should say most everyone followed the rules."

The room rang with laughter until Lana's voice brought a hush. "I plead the Fifth," she said, which revitalized the clamor.

Mark quieted the group. "Okay," he continued, "whose turn to say our blessing?"

When Janet raised her arm, Lana held her breath.

Mark's eyes widened, apparently as surprised as Lana. "Great. Janet volunteered."

He extended his arm toward Lana. She took his hand and offered her other hand to the person on the her right while the teens did the same, linking the entire room. To Lana's surprise when everyone bowed their heads, Janet began to sing. Her sweet, clear voice filled the room, and before she reached the second line, others had joined her.

They began a second verse, and by the end, even those who may not have known the song joined in the last line. Compliments filled the room when Janet finished, and Lana sent her own silent thanks to heaven as the girl graciously thanked those around her.

Lana studied the young people, different in many ways from her high school students. What made the difference? The answer struck her like a dart in a bull's-eye. God made the difference. These teens weren't afraid to demonstrate their faith. They acted out what God expected. Then she turned her thoughts inward. Did she? After these new experiences, Lana knew she had a place to start, and that would make the difference in her.

The Lord is good to me, Lana thought. *So good. And I don't deserve any of it, and that's what makes me all the more grateful.*

❧

Mark lay in his bunk and thought about the past week. The camp outing had helped him to become acquainted with the teens, and watching them grow in their relationships with Christ and each other had filled him with joy. What could be better in life than to be part of that experience?

With each new day, serving the Lord filled Mark with greater joy—a joy he couldn't explain—and feelings washed away his inner concern that he had made a bad career choice. God had strengthened his confidence.

To his great happiness, he'd gotten to know Lana even better. She brought smiles to his face with her abundant energy. . .though often that energy was aimed in the wrong direction. Somehow Mark sensed that God had directed him to her. Since they'd arrived at camp, he knew both he and Lana had changed in miraculous ways.

Struggling to fall asleep, Mark reviewed the ups and downs of the first week, reminding himself the last half of their stay began the next morning. After one silly prank in his cabin—a frog hidden in Jason's duffel bag—he had given the entire group a lecture on shaving cream in the sleeping bags and plastic wrap on the toilets. He'd planned ahead and prayed he'd thought of everything. At least, he hoped he had. Mark finally closed his eyes, looking forward to a fun-filled day the next morning.

During the night, the sound of heavy rain awakened Mark. Grateful that the camp had indoor activities if needed, he forced his eyes to stay closed, but within minutes, the heavens disturbed the silence. Cracks of lightning and the rumble of thunder jarred Mark again. Slipping out of his bunk, he tiptoed to the cabin window and peeked outside between the shutters.

A grand lightning display played above the soggy grass and rugged buildings. The dirt paths had turned to muddy rivers, and he wondered what the morning would hold.

"What's happening?" a voice asked from the darkness.

Mark heard the shuffle of a sleeping bag and then the patter of feet as the boy approached him.

In the light zigzagging through the window, Mark recognized Don. "Can't sleep?"

He shook his head. "At home noise like this is too familiar."

Though Lana had told Mark the boy's story, he shook his head as if he didn't understand.

Don explained about his family problems in a hushed whisper, limiting facts but getting the point across. "Coming here has been great." He leaned his back against the wall. "I needed friends, and when Miss W. . .when Lana invited me to come to church, I sloughed it off. But like I said before, something made me get up that morning, and I'll never be sorry."

"I'm glad," Mark said. "You've been a great addition to the camp."

"Thanks. I've made a lot of friends."

Mark nodded, giving the boy space to talk.

"You know what's really nice?" Don asked.

Mark rested his back against the wall and shook his head.

"Janet."

"Good company?" Mark asked, thinking of his feelings about Lana.

"That too, but she understands my problems. I guess that means more to me than anything. . .except the Bible studies. They've helped me focus on what's really important. Things won't be perfect at home, but I think I'll be able to handle it better."

Mark clasped the boy's shoulder. "That's the important thing, Don. You have friends and you have God. That makes life different."

The teen yawned and stretched. "Thanks," he said. "I've been wanting to say that."

"You're welcome," Mark said.

The boy smiled and then ambled back toward his bunk.

Mark stood in the window for a moment longer, and when fatigue pressed against his eyes, he returned to his bunk and drifted off to a restless sleep.

When dawn's light peeked between the shutter slats, Mark pulled himself up and sat on the edge of his bunk. The teens snored and mumbled in different stages of sleep, and he hated to rouse them to face the gloomy morning. He slid into his jeans and sneakers, then pulled a T-shirt over his head and crept toward the door. Moving in silence, he opened the door and slipped outside.

The rain had stopped, but the trees continued to drip, and rivulets of water ran where the pathway should have been. Across the sodden grass, Lana's cabin door opened, and she stepped outside, pulling the door closed behind her. From her expression, Mark knew without question that she had endured a difficult night.

When she saw him standing outside, she riveted her gaze to his and stepped from the wooden porch. Her hushed voice pierced the morning stillness as she headed toward him. "Latest on the home front. The roof leaks. Can you believe it?"

Mark opened his mouth to warn her about the slippery ground, but before he could act, Lana stepped from the grass, and her feet hit the sodden path and skidded in the muck. Wavering backward and forward like a child on her first ice skates, Lana struggled to retrieve her balance. With caution, Mark maneuvered through the mire, hoping to stop her fall, but before he'd taken three steps, Lana lay sprawled in a pool of mud. Her cry ricocheted through the trees, sending a bevy of birds flying heavenward.

When Mark reached her side, she looked like a chocolate-dipped bonbon. Mark sputtered between concern and laughter. "I tried, Lana." Fighting his amusement, his chuckle won out.

She glared up at him from her pitiful, prone position. "Don't just stand there. I'm up to my armpits in mud."

"I noticed." His chuckle gave way to a full laugh.

"Not funny, Mark." She extended her arm toward him for help.

Mark gripped her slippery fingers with a heave-ho, but instead, his feet did a heave-ho of their own, and he joined her, landing on his knees in the oozing muck. Facing her at eye level, he gawked at her soiled face. "Trying a mud pack? I hear they're great for a beautiful complexion."

"Really," she said, sending him a grin. "How about trying one yourself?" She lifted her muddy hands and dragged them across his cheeks.

They gaped at each other, and their laughter disturbed the quiet morning.

"Guess I fixed you," she said in her playful, cocky tone.

"Not as much as I fixed you."

"Fixed me?" Her face shuffled through a medley of confused expressions.

"It's morning. Men are scheduled to shower now. You'll have to wait until tonight, Missy." He raised himself, semi-covered in mud and helped Lana to stand.

"Please don't make me wait," she whined. "I can't go all day like this. You know—"

"Stop your pitiful moaning." He touched her nose with the tip of his finger, putting a daub of mud on one of the few spots that had remained unsullied. "Grab your clothes, and I'll stand guard."

"I could kiss you," she said. "Thanks."

As the words left her mouth, he watched surprise widen her eyes. "Not now, you can't," he said. Playfully, he stepped away from her mud-speckled form, yet longing to kiss her anyway, anytime. "Besides, I'm only doing this in hopes of getting another glimpse of your Howdy Doody bathrobe."

"Sorry," she said, wading back to her cabin, "that's at home in my treasure chest."

twelve

Clean again, Lana headed for breakfast. With a new appreciation for the cooks, she stopped complaining about the food and enjoyed listening to the conversation, jumping in when she had something to add. After the meal, the teens opted to stay in the activity hall until the sun dried the footpaths. Mark agreed, and the two parents offered to keep a watchful eye on the campers while they played Ping-Pong, darts, and board games.

Lana grinned at Mark, who looked cleaner and brighter than during their earlier meeting, and they slipped outside for a rare moment of free time. Wiser after their morning misadventure, they kept a watchful eye for slippery mud patches. As they headed toward the lake, Mark let his fingers brush against Lana's, and enjoying a rare moment alone with him, Lana eagerly slipped her fingers into his.

Enjoying the serenity, Lana regarded the rain-washed world—leaves and grass a shiny green. When they arrived at the lake, even the water rippled with a malachite glow. Ignoring the damp wood, Lana dropped to the park bench near the water's edge. In the glorious silence, neither she nor Mark spoke, but her mind drifted, and her heart thumped a tom-tom rhythm. She had fallen in serious "like" with the stray man her sister had dragged home only weeks earlier.

Though her heart drummed, Lana felt at peace. She'd been unhappy with herself for too long. Discontented at work and with her life in general, she'd looked at her sister with envy and irritation. Barb had learned an easy acceptance of herself and others long before Lana had even a vague understanding of what such an outlook meant. But now things were different.

Since she'd met Mark, a new feeling had emerged—a comfort with her faith and a completeness she'd never known before.

"Five bucks for your thoughts," Mark said, resting his arm along the bench back. His fingers played along her upper arm, and his touch sent tingles through her chest.

"Not worth a penny." She stopped herself. "Is my nose growing?"

"Only a little, Pinocchio."

She tilted her head and nodded. "My thoughts are worth a million dollars."

"Want to share?"

She did, but how? How could she say all that was in her heart without making herself uncomfortable and very vulnerable. He liked her, but did he feel the same as she? "It's hard to put my feelings into words. So much has happened these last few weeks." She gazed into his eyes. "Especially this past week."

"I've seen the difference. Felt the difference. Not only in you, but in me. I think God had His hand in our first meeting—as silly as that day was. Now that I think of it, you haven't attacked me with one power tool in the past couple of weeks."

Lana grinned. "Do you think God has a sense of humor?" The question sailed from her lips without her thinking, and she grimaced, fearing she had made light of the heavenly Father.

"I sure do. He made you. . . ."

Her head jerked upward, but her scowl faded when she saw his smiling face.

"And me," Mark continued. "We humans are a silly lot. I'm sure God gets a good laugh over our antics."

"And hurts with our pain," Lana added.

He nodded. "The Bible says Jesus wept."

His words wrapped around her heart. Jesus laughed and cried. The Lord knew human feelings and understood. The reality seemed overwhelming. "I've learned some things about myself at the camp." She tucked a lock of her hair behind her ear. "I'd like to think I'll be a better person one of these days."

"I'd like to think so too." He grinned at her.

She gave him a poke.

"You know I'm teasing. I have no right to judge anyone."

"What do you mean?" she said.

His playfulness faded, and he clasped her hand in his, caressing her knuckles with his free hand. "I spend a lot of time taunting you about being flawed and needing improvement, but I'm as flawed as anyone—and definitely need God's grace and guidance."

Her pulse skipped a beat before mounting to a trot. "I don't understand."

"I told you how God guided me to sign up for youth ministry classes."

Holding her breath, she nodded, fearing what he might tell her.

"I have spent a lot of time doubting God's wisdom, Lana. Even though I signed up for the classes and took a youth ministry job, I still questioned God. Still thought He'd made a mistake. Still figured I was unable—even more, unworthy—to guide young people." His gaze left hers and turned toward the blue water winking with sunshine.

She longed to respond, to tell him he was wrong, but wisdom guided her to listen.

"I learned something here too." He shifted his face toward hers, his gaze seeking the depths of her understanding. "I finally realized I don't have to be perfect. . .because God is perfect. All I have to do is help the teens struggle with that truth just like I have done all my life."

A deep sigh shot from Lana's chest. "It's that easy?"

"It's not easy," he said, grinning. "But it's the hard truth. If we give God the best we can by listening to the teens and speaking from our hearts, then we can't go wrong. Since I've been working with them these past months, I've always tried to ask myself how a Christian should handle the situation. In these past few days, I've questioned myself over and over."

She couldn't keep back her smile at seeing him so serious, but she loved seeing that side of him. "You make me laugh, Mark, and now. . .you've made me want to cry."

"Cry?"

"Because what you've said is so beautiful. . .and true.

"It's God talking, not me."

While she laughed, he slid his hand into his pocket and brought out a small package.

"Here," he said, handing it to her. "I bought you a little present before we left home."

Her heart skipped as she reached for the tiny paper bag. "Why did you do that?"

"I wanted to."

She slid her fingers into the sack and pulled out a thin, woven bracelet that displayed four letters: WWJD. She had no idea what it meant. Radio call letters was all that came to mind. "Christian radio station?"

His laugh filled the quiet. "You're kidding. Haven't you seen these? Teens wear them."

She shook her head, embarrassed that she'd never heard of the bracelets that apparently were popular with Christian teenagers.

"The letters stand for 'What would Jesus do?' I thought—"

"I can guess what you thought." She gave him a knowing smile and gazed at the bracelet resting in her fingers. "Thanks. Would you hook it for me?"

"Sure thing." He grasped the two ends and connected it around her wrist.

She studied the four letters. "This will be a great reminder. Lots better than a tattoo on my forehead. I know I'm not perfect, but I'm trying, and you've been a wonderful example for me."

"Me?" He shook his head. "You're looking at me through love's eyes."

The words startled them both, and their gazes locked.

Mark's tethered breath escaped him. "At least, I hope that's true."

His gaze drifted to her mouth, and Lana touched her bracelet and waited suspended as he leaned toward her. Eagerly, she lifted her lips to meet his, anticipating his kiss.

"Hey, there you are." A voice shot from the distance.

They jolted backward, Lana's heart tripping in expectation and disappointment like a ride on a roller coaster that climbs to the very edge of the first steep slope and stalls.

Looking as if he'd swallowed a chili pepper, Mark's face reddened, and he turned his head toward the voices. Behind them, two of the teens waved wildly, totally unaware they'd put a headlock on what Lana had hoped would be a very romantic moment.

Mark's rigid shoulders sagged. "Drat," he said. Then like a spy movie, before the teens arrived, he whispered in her ear. "I'll meet you after the team activity tonight. Behind your cabin. Nine o'clock."

Lana chuckled and pointed to her wrist. "Should we synchronize our watches?"

Playfully, they pushed their wrists together and compared minute and hour hands with a dramatic nod.

"Tonight," she murmured. "Nine o'clock."

When they lifted their eyes from their wrists, the teens had landed.

❧

The sun grew warmer as the day went on, and soon the grass no longer held traces of the morning's rain. After lunch, Mark began the Bible study. "Tonight, we're taking a deeper step in our studies. Two days ago, I tied you together with string, and you learned, I hope," he said, looking around the room at the grinning faces, "about cooperation. Without that, you'd still be strung together in knots."

The teens chuckled and groaned as they remembered their feeble attempts to avoid breaking the string while getting untied.

"Tonight, we have two events, one with string and one without."

Moans were quickly followed by applause.

"Before I tell you about tonight's activities, let's open our Bibles to Luke 6:39–40. Jesus has been answering questions, and we know how Jesus often explains his meanings."

"Through parables," Gary said.

"Absolutely, and after Jesus told the questioners a parable, this is what he said." Mark looked down at the Bible and read: " 'Can a blind man lead a blind man? Will they not both fall into a pit? A student is not above his teacher, but everyone who is fully trained will be like his teacher.' "

An intense discussion followed. Some wondered how it would feel to be blind, and others tried to comprehend how they could be a student, yet a teacher.

"Tonight, you'll find answers to both these questions," Mark said. "Give it some thought as you enjoy your day."

ঽ৶

With the day growing hot and sunny, just about everyone gathered at the beach that afternoon, though Lana had no desire to swim in what she considered frog- and snake-infested water. The young people splashed and bounded in the lake while the adults watched from the shore.

When the two parents headed for the rowboat, Mark slid next to Lana. "What time does your watch say?" he asked, a silly grin playing on his face.

"Two-thirty. How about you?" Lana's pulse tripped at his smile.

"Same." He leaned his head sideways and pressed it against

hers for a fleeting minute.

She longed for the hours to pass so she could experience their comical secret rendezvous.

Mark looked back out toward the water. "Only four more days and we're heading home."

Lana's heart sank like a stone. Though crawling into her own cozy bed at home sounded wonderful, she would miss the special time they'd shared here. "You sound disappointed," she said, hoping to hear he felt the same.

"Disappointed? Not at all." He didn't flinch but stared ahead.

Lana struggled to keep her disappointment hidden.

Slowly, he turned to face her, his expression taunting. "I'll have my own bed to sleep in and get back to my everyday, lonely routine. No irritable woman to ruin my scrambled eggs or knock me into the mud."

"Right. And no more leaky roofs, canoe disasters, or creepy, crawling, slithering things."

His teasing eyes softened. "I'll miss being together like this."

A sigh ruffled through her. "Me too," she admitted.

"I know we don't live too far apart, but it's not quite the same. Life gets busy, and you'll probably find excuses to avoid me."

"Avoid you? Not me." She paused. "If I did, you'd probably miss my antics."

He caressed her fingers. "You make me laugh."

"At or with?" she asked.

His forehead wrinkled in a thoughtful scowl.

"Laugh at me or with me?"

His expression shifted to a grin. "Aren't they the same?"

She gave him a poke. "Not in my head they aren't."

His gaze sought hers and hung there, suspended. "You're learning to laugh at yourself, and I'm learning to care so much for you."

Her heartbeat did a Texas two-step and then galloped ahead like her wild ride on Fury, leaving her breathless. She could only nod, acknowledging the truth. She'd changed in the past few days. More than she could ever imagine.

All Lana thought about the rest of the day was the evening's private meeting with Mark. Why, she wasn't sure. So far, their best intentions had turned to lumpy oatmeal, but her pulse raced in anticipation anyway. After dinner she ambled outside, wandering alone while Mark explained the team activities.

When the teens gathered on the grass, Mark blindfolded four at a time and gave them a lengthy piece of string tied at the ends. "Your job is to form this string into a square."

"How?" Don asked, peeking from beneath the cloth binding his eyes.

"No peeking," Mark said, tugging the fabric in place. "The first step is to discuss the solution between yourselves. Then move around until you think you've accomplished it." He turned and looked at the others watching. "No hints from the crowd, and avoid sounds—especially laughter. Let them do this on their own."

The group agreed. The four teens stood in the middle while the others formed a large circle around them. Those blindfolded pondered and discussed how to shape a square. Each one tried to convince the others his way was best. Finally, they settled on a system and moved into position.

Lana grinned, seeing the lopsided shape they'd formed.

"Take off the blindfold," Mark said.

When they removed the covering from their eyes, all the teens joined in the laughter.

"It's impossible," Jason said.

Mark shook his head. "Wait. Let's see if it is."

They discussed where they went wrong, and four more blindfolded teenagers set out to learn from their fellow campers' mistakes. The result was not much better.

Lana watched with interest, impressed by how Mark had set up the exercise.

The next four had help—a group of teens who had already discussed the best way to accomplish the task. While the four held the string, blindfolded, Teri, serving as the group captain, called out instructions about where each should move and when. The result was a near perfect square.

After the cheers quieted, Mark stepped into the center. "So what's the lesson?"

"Don't try to accomplish things on your own. Ask for help," Gary said.

"When you do ask for help, listen to instructions and follow them," Susan added.

Don raised his arm. "Sometimes we can't accomplish things alone because we're knocked over by the problems and blind to the solutions. But someone else, who can see what we can't, can help us."

The meaning became clear, and the teens talked about their need for Jesus' friendship and for the Holy Spirit's guidance.

Lana contemplated the discussion. *Sometimes we can't accomplish things alone because we're blind to the solutions.* Don's words reverberated in her mind. She needed to say the phrase over and over until it stayed with her.

When the team lessons were finished, the teens had free time until lights out. Mark and Lana ambled away and headed for their cabins, waiting to make sure the teens were occupied before their rendezvous.

Dusk had settled over the woods, and darkness was not far behind. When Lana's wristwatch read nine o'clock, she slipped outside and rounded the corner for the darkest area behind her cabin.

The heat of the day had melted into a pleasantly warm evening. In the moonlit darkness, the heady scent of decaying undergrowth enveloped her. She listened for Mark's footsteps, but only the lone hoot of an owl and distant croaking of the frogs broke the stillness.

Finally, a rustle of brush drew her attention, and she waited hidden in the shadows. A familiar silhouette rounded the cabin.

"Lana?"

"I'm here." She moved toward him, feeling giddy. "This is silly, isn't it?"

"Oh, I don't know. Getting away from this pack of kids isn't easy." He paused a moment. "Let's take a walk toward the archery range. We should be alone there. Notice I said 'should be.' " He drew her alongside him.

Lana moved with careful steps in the dark to avoid turning her ankle in the rutted underbrush. "Do you feel like a Hardy boy out on a caper?"

His chuckle sounded rich in the quiet night. "More like Davy Crockett sneaking up on the Indians."

"And I'm an Indian chief's daughter," she said, joining his game, "like—"

"Princess Summerfall Winterspring."

She cringed. "Please. Not back to Howdy Doody!"

He slid his arm around her shoulder, drawing her closer. With a spurt of courage Lana wrapped her arm around Mark's waist. The hay bales used for targets at the archery range appeared as silhouettes in the moonlight, and when Mark and Lana reached them, he lifted her into the air as easily as a downy pillow and set her on top, then scooted up next to her and placed his arm around her waist.

She nuzzled close to his side. "This camping thing has been wonderful, and so many things about it. Enjoying the setting, the Bible study. . .and you."

He drew her closer. "It has been special." His voice sounded husky in her ear.

She loved being nestled in his arms. "And the kids," she

added. "I've really enjoyed getting to know them."

"It's obvious you care about the teens. Remember the things you said when we first met?"

She shook her head. "I bet you wondered what kind of a horrible person I was."

"No," he remained thoughtful. "I realized that you needed to focus on God's will and ask the Holy Spirit for help. It worked. Look how you were with Janet. You forgot about your own needs and helped her when she needed a friend."

"She's like a new kid in just over a week. Almost a miracle."

"It's not the amount of time, Lana. It's the heart. And it's God working in that heart. That's what makes the difference."

"And that's what's changed me."

"God working in your heart?"

For a moment, she could only nod. Tears pushed against the back of her eyes, and she wiped them away, glad that the darkness hid her emotion. "I've been a Christian most all of my life. A Christian in name, that is, but I need to work harder to live my life the way God expects."

And so did he. With his arms around Lana's shoulder, Mark felt tension rifle through her. She gazed at him in the moonlight, and moisture glinted in her eyes. He shifted and kneaded the tension in her neck.

She flexed her shoulders and moved her head from side to side. "That feels so good."

He harnessed his emotion. If that line wasn't the perfect lead-in, nothing was. "If you think that feels good, this should feel wonderful."

He guided his fingers from her neck to the tip of her chin and tilted her mouth toward his. Her lips looked firm and inviting in the creamy moonlight, and he moved his palm across her hair as his lips touched hers.

Their unison sigh rose and met like voices blending in harmony. . .and Mark loved the song they sang. He eased his mouth tenderly from hers, and as he spoke he felt the feathery touch of his lips near hers. "I've wanted to kiss you like this all day."

"And I've wanted—"

"Mark. Lana. Where are you?" Voices shot through the darkness, turning their melody into caterwauling.

"I know they came this way," a female voice muttered.

Instinctively, Lana and Mark dove from the hay and crouched behind the bales. Mark inched along, staying low to the ground, and Lana followed. They crisscrossed their way back into the trees through the tall grass like video-game characters.

"They're great kids," Mark muttered, "but I wanted just a few moments alone with you."

"I know."

Youthful voices swept across the field. "Did you see them?" asked one teen. "Over that way," said another. "Hey, let's leave Mark alone," hissed a different voice.

Mark lowered himself into the grass, then inched his way into the woods. Lana followed behind him. "I'm the youth director," he whispered over his shoulder. "What am I doing?"

When the night seemed quiet again, Mark stopped, leaned his back against a tree, and pulled Lana to him. "Aren't we terrible? I feel like a kid hiding from my parents."

Lana shook her head. "I know. I feel guilty—like we've done something wrong."

Turning her around to face him, Mark clasped her to him. "Instead we've done something right."

Hand-in-hand, they wandered the long way back and arrived at the shimmering lake drenched with moonlight. Sitting on the bench, Mark brushed her cheek with his fingertips. "We won't forget this night, will we?"

"Never," Lana said, with a loving sigh.

thirteen

In the middle of the night, Lana realized the words she'd said earlier in the evening had been the absolute truth. She would never forget that night. Yet there was more than Mark's wonderful kiss that woke her in the darkness. Her legs and arms itched as if they'd been attacked by a herd of mosquitoes in a roundup. She pointed her flashlight beneath the sheet and witnessed the telltale blisters dotting her lower legs and arms where she'd crawled through the underbrush.

Though irritated with herself, she couldn't hold back a chuckle, thinking of Mark scratching himself into a tizzy in his cabin. She reviewed what she might have brought along in her luggage to stop the stinging. Nothing came to mind. *Great planning, Miss Organization!* Yet somewhere in the cabin she recalled seeing some pink lotion.

She tiptoed from her bed and crept along the rows of bunks, gazing at the window sills. That's where she'd seen it. Sure enough, the silhouette of a bottle glowed in the moonlight, and stealthily she pulled it from its narrow sill and eased her way outside.

She headed for the bathroom, where a light glowed, and inside she gawked down at her red blistered limbs. Smoothing the pink fluid onto her arms and legs, she wondered whose parent had been wise enough to send the healing balm along. After sealing the bottle, she whipped outside and, in the darkness, missed seeing the hurtling body who charged into her, leaving her breathless.

She stood for a moment to catch her wind, and Mark gazed down at her, dumbfounded. "I'm miserable. I've been itching for hours," he grumbled. Then he glanced at her arms sticking from beneath her T-shirt. "You too?"

She nodded with a guilty smile. "Up to my neck."

He yawned and gaped at her. "What should we do now?"

"Want to borrow some of this lotion? I found it on a window sill. I feel better already."

"I suppose. Anything is better than this. I'm a mess," he grumbled.

Lana opened the bottle and daubed some of the soothing lotion on the spots bubbling up on his arms and legs.

Unexpectedly, Mark pulled away from her. "Wait a minute," he said, staring at the thickly coated spots. "I can't wear pink. Pink's for girls."

Lana sputtered. "You can't? Well, sorry, but this doesn't come in blue. Pink is the fashion color of the season."

"Then go easy. Not such big globs."

To taunt him, she made the next spots bigger than before. He grimaced but didn't complain.

Lana screwed the lid closed. "I don't know whose lotion this is, but I'll explain in the morning."

"Do you think you could leave my name out of it? We'll look a bit suspicious with our arms and legs covered in pink goop."

"Don't be a baby, Mark. I'll tell them a masked bandit crawled through the poison ivy with me." She gave him the once-over and snickered. "You can sneak a second coating under your clothes in the morning. Stop whining." She tiptoed and gave him a teensy kiss on the lips.

With the pretense of drama, he staggered backward. "Now that makes this all worthwhile." His mouth curved into his sunny smile.

Lana smirked and ignored his comment. Without a word, they turned back toward their individual cabins and waved a silent good night.

❧

Mark returned to bed and had to admit that the lotion did ease the terrible itching. He envisioned the scene and chuckled to himself. They did make a silly sight, each of them dotted with pink spots covering their blistering skin. He should have known better than to creep along the ground. Poison ivy and poison oak were the first plants he'd learned about in Camping 101. But at that moment, he'd been desperate. Stifling his overtired snickers, he tried to close his eyes.

But his thoughts returned to Lana. They'd almost had time to talk about things that were important until his youthful charges interrupted them. Mark longed for some quiet time to share his dreams and hopes with the woman who'd barreled into his heart. The sensation had caught him way off guard.

Still amazed, he relived how his feelings had run away with him. He was no kid anymore. He'd be thirty on his next birthday. Then his mind drifted, wondering at what age wisdom became one of God's gifts. Or if he might ever be wise. But tonight—except for his telltale blisters—he felt a little smarter.

For the first time in his life, he knew positively that he'd made the right career decision. He felt at home with these teens. Sure, he wanted to have a moment of quiet, but he loved what he was doing. Each day, he grew stronger in his faith and worked to improve his weaknesses. He felt blessed to be given the task of touching their young lives with pure, clean enjoyment and with Bible study and fellowship, despite his personal flaws.

Those experiences still lived inside him from his own youth. He prayed that these teens would come away from the experience with memories that made a difference. With Lana on his mind and his itching limbs soothed, he finally drifted off to sleep.

The early morning sun shot through the window and pressed against his eyes. The itching had roused itself as morning neared, and Mark jumped out of his bunk, slid on his clothes, and darted across the grass. He needed some of Lana's medicine. And he needed it before the whole camp awoke.

With only a light tap on the window, Lana heard him and tiptoed to the door. She opened it a crack and poked the bottle outside. "And hurry up. I don't want to wake the girls."

"What's wrong, Lana?" One of the girls' voices mumbled, as she lifted her head and gaped through the doorway.

"Nothing, Sara," Lana whispered back. "Go to sleep."

"Is that Mark outside?" the girl hissed.

"Shush, I don't want you to wake the others." Lana warned her again.

"I'm already awake." Janet's voice sailed through the doorway. "What's wrong?"

"Nothing," Lana said, hoping they'd go back to sleep.

"Then what's all the commotion about?" Susan asked.

Janet leaned over her bunk and peeked through the chink in the door. "Mark's using calamine lotion. Poison ivy?"

Lana held her finger to her lips to silence her and nodded. Janet's gaze traveled down Lana's arm, staring at her telltale blisters also caked with the pink lotion. A grin rose on the girl's lips. "I think you two better find a safer place to chat than in a poison ivy patch."

A loud yawn traveled along the bunks. "Who has poison ivy?" Teri asked.

A muffled voice rose from a sleeping bag. "Lana and Mark. Our fearless leaders."

A snicker traveled the length of the room.

Lana shook her head. "Don't call me your fearless leader. This is the first camping trip of my life, and I don't plan to go on another one—ever."

"Oh, you'd better not say that," Janet murmured. "Mark's a youth director. He'll have lots of camping trips to take in his lifetime. And I think he'll want you right there at his side."

Lana felt a flush cover her cheeks. "Hush." But the truth was she wanted to be at his side—forever.

Girlish giggles filled the cabin.

"Look," someone snickered. "She's blushing."

Mark stuck the bottle through the gap in the doorway.

Instead of taking the container, Lana flung the door open wide. "No sense in being subtle, Mark. They're all in here laughing at us hysterically."

He gaped at them helplessly and then grinned. "Okay, but one word from any of you, and I'll. . .I'll. . ."

"You'll what?" Lana asked.

"I'll think of something."

"It's cute, Mark," Janet called from her bunk. "You and Lana look really great together. Especially with both of you decorated in pink."

Mark raised his eyebrows and glared at the girl. "The lotion doesn't come in blue, Janet. I asked."

Eight girls sat up in their bunks and joined in a full-bodied laugh as he spun on his heel and headed back to his cabin.

❧

Mark leaned against a bench near the dining hall, waiting for the lunch bell. He felt hungry. In fact, more than ready to eat. "These two weeks have turned me into a trash compactor. I'm never full."

"Nervous energy," Lana agreed. "Keeping an eye on thirty-two teens isn't cotton candy."

"No, but they sure tried to stick to us as if we were." Mark let loose a chuckle, thinking of his analogy, then glanced at his drying blisters. "Three days with that lotion and we're lookin' good." He beamed a smile her way.

Lana surveyed her arms and legs. "I thanked Sara for the calamine. Glad her mother thought ahead. But I worried we might spread the infection all over the place."

Mark grinned. "No, but we did an A-one job on ourselves."

"And taught everyone an important lesson at the same time. Don't walk through underbrush in the dark." She gave him her teacher expression. "Always remember to turn your bungled activities into a positive experience."

"I suppose when you put it that way. . ."

Lana pulled herself into a ramrod pose. "I'm the master of bungling."

Mark laughed at her confession. "No one could argue that."

As the words left his mouth, the lunch bell rang, and the crowd appeared like a tidal wave and filled the dining hall. With a clatter of forks and knives, the campers finished lunch, and before they scattered, Mark knew he'd better review their final day.

"Quiet everyone." His voice resounded through the room, and little by little, the din dwindled. "Free time this afternoon to enjoy yourselves. But remember we leave tomorrow so you may want to gather your things together and not leave it all until morning. After dinner, we'll have our final Bible study and then our farewell bonfire. So when you're done here, you're free to go. . .but stay out of trouble."

Amid their hoots and chuckles, an arm shot up. Mark pivoted toward the teenager. "Dennis?"

The teen's discomfort was evident as he squirmed in his chair. "Teri didn't show for lunch. I wondered if anyone's seen her."

Mark recalled seeing the pair as a constant twosome, so the young man's words sent a minor charge through his chest. "Anyone? Girls? Is Teri still in her cabin?"

Lana touched his arm. "She wasn't there just before I came outside. She bunks in my cabin."

Mark's pulse picked up pace. "Anyone?"

The teens stared with blank expressions toward him. As they rose to leave, Mark figured he'd better get down to the facts. "Hold up, Dennis."

Before he headed toward the youth, Sara stepped up. "I heard Teri say earlier she was going down by the lake."

Lana pressed the teen's shoulder. "Thanks, Sara, we'll have a look."

Dennis came forward, guilt written over his face, making Mark more than curious. "What's up, Dennis?"

He shrugged. "Teri and I had a little argument this morning, and she huffed off. I thought she'd get over it and I could talk with her at lunch, but—"

"But she's not here, so you're worried." He lifted an eyebrow at the teen.

Dennis nodded.

"Mark," Lana said, "did you hear Sara?"

He turned his eyes toward Lana. "The lake?"

Lana nodded.

"Then we'd better check it out."

The three rushed down toward the lake and met Sara heading back. Before they reached her, she called to them. "She's not there, and the rowboat's there so she didn't take it out."

Jolted by nervous energy, Mark gathered his wits. He had prayed nothing would go wrong on this trip. Now, on their last day, he looked heavenward. *Lord, keep each of these kids safely in Your care.* He eased his rigid shoulders back, letting God's promise filter through him—Ask, and you shall receive. Mark struggled to let go and receive.

He looked into three tense faces. "Okay, let's think logically and then spread out. Lana, check your cabin, toilet, and shower. Sara, you check the other girls' cabins and the activity hall. Dennis and I will cover the archery range and soccer fields, then the hiking trails. We'll meet back here, hopefully with Teri. Okay?"

❧

As Lana darted into the cabin, her mind flew. What does an angry teenage girl do? Usually something dramatic, she remembered from her own youth. The cabin was quiet, as were the two outbuildings. Dramatic? What was dramatic?

She spun around. She might pin herself to the archery bull's-eye, but the guys were checking there. Lana closed her eyes. The lake made sense, and Lana raced back to the water's edge. It made a great setting for moping and feeling sorry for one's self. She'd done it herself as a teen.

Lana's legs prodded her to the lake almost faster than she could run. Disappointment washed over her when she skidded to a stop. No one. The rowboat sat empty at the shoreline. She sat on the bench, resting her elbows on her knees, and thought. A canoe? Teri wouldn't go out alone in a canoe. Dramatic, yes. But foolish.

Her heartbeat charged to a sprinter's pace, and Lana rushed to the far side of the boat shed. The door gaped open, and a deep rut had been cut through the loose sand where a canoe had been dragged to the water. Sure enough, the foolish, lovesick teen had gone off alone in a canoe. Lana looked back toward the cabins far in the distance. Should she waste time looking for help or go on her own? The question surprised her. Her take-charge attitude faltered.

A "no time to spare" intuition ran through her, and she pulled at a canoe, amazed they were heavier than she expected. She tugged it with amazing strength to the water's edge, then darted back for two paddles. She pushed the canoe carefully into the water. Where it rested against the sand, she stepped into the center, remembering as many of the rules as she could. This time, not standing up, she crouched and worked her way to the middle. But at that moment, she faltered.

She should leave Mark a message. She glanced down at her bracelet. WWJD. If she left that on the beach, he'd know where she was. With caution, she stepped from the canoe and darted across the sand to the bench. She tugged on the bracelet, then paused. What would Jesus do? The question slowed her thoughts. Jesus would pray. . .and He'd look to His disciples for help. The awareness struck her.

What had Mark been teaching the teens during the two weeks? Teamwork. Cooperation. Not depending on yourself but turning to others and to God. Though she knew God would be with her, she couldn't go alone. If she'd learned one thing during these two weeks, she'd learned to listen to others. She had to be patient and get help.

Lana pushed her feet through the sand, then reached hard ground where running came easier. In a moment, she saw one of the teens heading toward her. "Gary," she waved her arm. "Tell the others she took a canoe. Tell Mark I'll start out and for him to follow."

He gave her an understanding wave and spun around, heading back toward the cabins.

Thanking God for reminding her to rely on others, Lana turned back and climbed into the canoe. Once settled, she dug the canoe paddle into the water and tugged with her short arms. Slowly she moved into the lake and finally caught the river current. If she hadn't left word for Mark, she would have no idea how to get back to camp, fighting against the current's surprising strength. Now she knew Mark would be on his way to help her.

"Oh, help me, Lord," Lana called out aloud. "I need Your guidance. Teri's in deep trouble." The words might have made her smile another day, but at this moment Lana saw nothing to grin about. Her skills at people-saving had never been tested.

The current helped her move along, and the lessons from the earlier canoe trip had apparently found a home in her brain. She moved the paddle from one side to the other, pushing the water past her, digging deep and gaining speed.

Lana glanced over her shoulder. The lake was far behind, but she thought she saw a speck where the beach area had vanished around the bend. Mark. Her head leaped with hope. Ahead, she saw nothing but water and sky and the shoreline on each side of the fast-rolling river. Approaching a parcel of trees along the shore, she recognized the place where she'd fallen into the water days earlier. She steered clear of the spot, but around the next bend, her heart lurched. A canoe paddle lay captured in the tangle of tree branches.

"Teri! Teri! Are you there?" She searched the bank for evidence. Tears rolled from her eyes, and she launched fervent prayers to heaven. Along the bank, she spotted an overturned canoe. Her senses jolted as a young voice sailed to her over the water. "Here. I'm over here."

Lana looked ahead and caught sight of the teenager, waving wildly from the bank a few yards ahead. She looked behind and saw the distant form growing larger. A mixture of relief and fear plummeted through Lana's chest. *What could have happened, Lord? But You kept her safe. Thank You.*

"I'm coming!" Lana called. Calling out words of assurance to the teenager, her voice rose on the breeze as she pulled herself toward the shore. But Lana's panic remained. If that speck behind her wasn't Mark, what would they do? She had no idea.

Teri hung over the bank and grabbed the end of the canoe. "I was so stupid," the teen uttered over and over. "Just because I was upset at Dennis. And it was so silly."

"He's already forgiven you, Teri, and he's scared to death."

"He is?" she asked, clinging to Lana's side.

"He sure is."

Lana held the shivering girl in her arms, hoping her own tremors would go unnoticed. She looked down the lonely stretch of river, wondering how she'd had the stamina to get this far and praying that Mark's strong arms would bring him to her quickly. Then her eyes lifted to heaven, and peace filled her.

fourteen

Mark's chest tightened as fear gripped him. They'd searched everywhere. When the campers reassembled to compare notes, everyone gathered except Lana and Gary. Now his panic heightened. Others had joined the hunt to no avail. He closed his eyes, trying to imagine where the two had gone. As independent as Lana was, he had no way of guessing what she had done.

Before he could calculate what to do, Gary appeared, running toward them. "She took a canoe. Lana's on her way and asked you to follow."

Following Gary, the group ran toward the lake. Mark's mind whirred, praising God Lana hadn't gone off without asking for help.

"Okay, the rest of you wait here. Keep your eyes open while Dennis and I take the rowboat."

The parents gathered the teens around them in animated chatter as Mark and Dennis rowed away from shore.

The boat glided along quickly, picking up the river current. With powerful tugs of the oars, they sailed past the shoreline, eyes peeled for any sign of either canoe. As they rounded the bend, a canoe paddle bobbed among the debris at the bank, but they pressed forward.

Mark saw them before Dennis and waved his arms wildly. Relief charged through him when both women waved back, and their shouts of encouragement bounced across the water.

When they reached shore, Mark jumped to the sand to moor the boat, and before he reached Lana, she froze in place, and her piercing scream sent a bevy of frightened birds fluttering from the trees.

His heart lodged in his throat, and he charged toward her while Lana's face paled in horror.

"It's only a snake," Teri yelled, tugging on Lana's arm.

Mark masked his grin. Lana had met her nemesis. She shot across the grass like an arrow and, in a heartbeat, clung to Mark's chest.

He wrapped his arm around her shaking frame. "You're okay now. It's gone. You scared the snake worse than he scared you, Lana."

"Are you sure it's gone?" she asked, her head buried in his shirt.

"Positive." He chuckled silently. "You're safe from snakes and being marooned."

She lifted her head from his chest. "Praise the Lord you found us. I had no idea what to do," Lana whispered, her body still trembling.

Mark tightened his embrace. "You did the right thing. You ran for help." He tilted his head lower to gaze into her eyes.

"I was positive Teri had taken a canoe, and I almost left without sending word to you." Her face flushed with her guilty admission.

"But you didn't. You asked for help and then went after her. Two weeks ago you'd have suggested someone else look for Teri."

Lana's eyes widened. "You're right. I probably would have done just that." A sad grin tugged at her mouth. "You know what did it?"

"Did it?" He studied her face, wondering what she meant.

"What reminded me to go for help?"

Whatever it was, he thanked God for the blessing.

She lifted her arm. "The bracelet. WWJD. I started to leave the bracelet on the bench, thinking you'd find it, but instead, I thought of the meaning. This gift means more to me than you'll ever know."

A large lump caught in Mark's throat. He hadn't cried in years, not since he was a kid, but maybe tears weren't so bad. If they were good enough for Jesus, they were good enough for him. He wiped the moisture from his eyes and sent an inner prayer of thanksgiving heavenward. A prayer thanking God for the women's safety and for Lana's growth.

ఎ.

Mark looked over the crowd after dinner, their faces a blend of emotions. In the morning they would return home to the comforts they enjoyed, and the good times they'd shared would be only memories. Mark felt the same. His gaze settled on Lana's thoughtful face. He'd given thanks so many times during the day for Lana and Teri's safety. Lana had changed his life.

The activity hall seemed warm, and a breeze had risen outside. Rather than keep the campers inside, Mark suggested having Bible study around their last campfire. The teens accepted his idea with eagerness.

While the evening was still light, they ambled in, two and three at a time, and gathered around the fire pit. As he scanned their faces, his gaze settled on Lana in the dusky light, looking up at him from the log, her face tanned and her tousled hair streaked with sunny highlights. His chest burst with happiness.

He opened the Bible and scanned the verse, sensing the message was a perfect way to end the camping trip. "First let's think back over our two weeks together. As I watched you these past days, I've seen the closeness and warmth that have happened in the short time we've been together. Imagine if we could reach out to the world with the same zeal. How wonderful the earth would be."

Murmurs of agreement drifted across the open space.

"We've worked on communication and cooperation, all part of teamwork. And I hope we've developed a bond with each other and an even greater one with the Lord. When we go home, keep what you learned in your thoughts. The enjoyment and experiences will soon be only memories, but I hope the lessons we learned have planted seeds in your hearts."

His eyes shifted again to Lana, her sweet face gazing at him with open admiration. He loved her, and all he needed was the courage to tell her so.

He turned again to the Scriptures and eyed the waiting teens. "For those who have their Bibles, open them to Galatians 5:22–25. The rest of you can listen. I hope you will take these verses with you and keep them close. They will serve as a personal motto for each of us as we return home: 'But the fruit of the Spirit is love, joy, peace, patience, kindness, goodness, faithfulness, gentleness and self-control. Against such things there is no law. Those who belong to Christ Jesus have crucified the sinful nature with its passions and desires. Since we live by the Spirit, let us keep in step with the Spirit.' "

Rather than discuss the passage, he asked the teens to think quietly about what he'd read. After a few minutes of silence, he closed with prayer.

To his surprise, the teens had prepared their own words of thanks. Gary rose, and as he reminisced their two weeks together, his wit and good spirit infected everyone as quickly as the poison ivy Mark and Lana had endured. Laughter lifted as high as the smoke from the bonfire.

"If you're having marshmallows tonight," Lana added, "please don't show me your perfect specimen." She sent out a warm smile and was greeted with more merriment.

"How's your poison ivy, Mark?" Don asked.

"And how's yours, Lana?" Janet teased.

Lana grinned, but Mark nailed them with his witty remark. "If all of you had learned to leave a man and woman alone for a few minutes so they could have a serious conversation, no one would have poison ivy, and who knows what special moments might have happened?"

Kissing sounds echoed around the campfire and ended only

when the sound of guitar music filled the air. The campers joined in with familiar camp songs while Mark settled beside Lana, and in the dark, they clasped hands. Scanning the teens, he noticed Janet sat close to Don, and once again, Dennis and Teri smiled at each other, their squabble resolved. As the moon rose and the fire died, Mark sent the teens back to the cabins, herded along by the two counselors. Standing in the silence, Mark looked at Lana and drew in a deep, relieved breath.

"Should we douse the fire?" Lana asked, feeling a surge of comfort wash over her.

Mark nodded, and he shoveled sand onto the smoldering ashes while Lana raked the coals that had drifted away back into the pit.

As she pulled on the rake, Lana looked down at her blue and white WWJD bracelet—what would Jesus do? Mark couldn't have given her a more appropriate gift. The bracelet would help keep her on track.

With a final bucket of sand sprinkled over the charred wood, Mark stepped back and caught Lana's hand. "So this is it? Tomorrow, we're home."

Courage and honesty rushed through Lana's thoughts. "I'm home right now, Mark." His moonlit smile brightened the darkness, and her heart swelled with complete joy. "This has been some camping trip."

"Lana, I wish I could tell you what it's meant to me. You've been a partner through it all. A difficult partner at times, but a perfect partner. I thank God for bringing us together."

She grinned. "Maybe we should thank Barb too. She brought you home."

"When we first got here, I figured we'd leave after two weeks with you not speaking to me. Instead, I've fallen in love with you. I hope you know that."

She tried to speak, but her voice caught in her throat, and she only nodded.

He slipped his arm around her and drew her closer to his side. "I think of all the crazy things that happened. You were up to your elbows in soapsuds, waist-deep in frogs, up to—"

"Up to my neck in poison ivy." She gazed into his glowing, moonlit eyes and smiled. "And now I'm over my head in love." She looked into the spangled sky and sensed God's blessing.

Mark's gaze embraced her. "I love you with all my heart, Lana, and there's nothing better in the whole world than to be loved."

As naturally as the sun rising, their lips met, and Lana's heart soared over her head and up toward the stars. Like them, she glimmered with happiness, and she silently praised God for His generous blessing—the gift of love.

A Letter To Our Readers

Dear Reader:

In order that we might better contribute to your reading enjoyment, we would appreciate your taking a few minutes to respond to the following questions. We welcome your comments and read each form and letter we receive. When completed, please return to the following:

Rebecca Germany, Fiction Editor
Heartsong Presents
PO Box 719
Uhrichsville, Ohio 44683

1. Did you enjoy reading *Over Her Head* by Gail Gaymer Martin?

☐ Very much! I would like to see more books by this author!

☐ Moderately. I would have enjoyed it more if

_____

_____

2. Are you a member of **Heartsong Presents**?   Yes ☐   No ☐
If no, where did you purchase this book?_____ _____

_____

3. How would you rate, on a scale from 1 (poor) to 5 (superior), the cover design?_____

4. On a scale from 1 (poor) to 10 (superior), please rate the following elements.

_____ Heroine   _____ Plot

_____ Hero   _____ Inspirational theme

_____ Setting   _____ Secondary characters

5. These characters were special because_____

_____

_____

6. How has this book inspired your life?_____

_____

_____

7. What settings would you like to see covered in future
   Heartsong Presents books?_____

_____

_____

8. What are some inspirational themes you would like to see
   treated in future books?_____

_____

_____

9. Would you be interested in reading other **Heartsong
   Presents** titles?   Yes ❏   No ❏

10. Please check your age range:
    ❏ Under 18   ❏ 18-24   ❏ 25-34
    ❏ 35-45   ❏ 46-55   ❏ Over 55

Name _____

Occupation _____

Address _____

City _____ State _____ Zip _____

Email _____

MONTANA

Montanans are legendary for their courage and willingness to take on challenges as big as the Montana sky. But the heroines in these four inspirational novels are ordinary people facing mountains of trouble. As the comforts of daily routine are threatened, they'll need to dig deep for a sustaining faith.

Set in the fictional town of Rocky Bluff, Montana, these four complete contemporary novels by author Ann Bell demonstrate the power of prayer, friendship, and love.

MONTANA SKIES

In this follow-up to the best-selling book *Montana*, the legacy of Edith Harkness infuses the fictional town of Rocky Bluff, where four young women will learn the power of prayer and unconditional love.

In Montana Skies, author Ann Bell tells the compelling stories of four women in need, one woman who intercedes, and a love that could be just a prayer away.

paperback, 464 pages, 5 ¾₆" x 8"

♥ ♥ ♥ ♥ ♥ ♥ ♥ ♥ ♥ ♥ ❤ ♥ ♥ ♥ ♥ ♥ ♥ ♥ ♥

Please send me _____ copies of *Montana* and _____ copies of *Montana Skies*. I am enclosing $6.97 for each book ordered. (Please add $2.00 to cover postage and handling per order. OH add 6% tax.)

Send check or money order, no cash or C.O.D.s please.

Name_____

Address _____

City, State, Zip _____

To place a credit card order, call 1-800-847-8270.
Send to: Heartsong Presents Reader Service, PO Box 721, Uhrichsville, OH 44683

♥ ♥ ♥ ♥ ♥ ♥ ♥ ♥ ♥ ❤ ♥ ♥ ♥ ♥ ♥ ♥ ♥ ♥

Heart♥ng

CONTEMPORARY ROMANCE IS CHEAPER BY THE DOZEN!

Any 12 Heartsong Presents titles for only $27.00*

Buy any assortment of twelve *Heartsong Presents* titles and save 25% off of the already discounted price of $2.95 each!

*plus $2.00 shipping and handling per order and sales tax where applicable.

HEARTSONG PRESENTS *TITLES AVAILABLE NOW:*

(If ordering from this page, please remember to include it with the order form.)

·······Presents·······

Great Inspirational Romance at a Great Price!

Heartsong Presents books are inspirational romances in contemporary and historical settings, designed to give you an enjoyable, spirit-lifting reading experience. You can choose wonderfully written titles from some of today's best authors like Hannah Alexander, Irene B Brand, Yvonne Lehman, Tracie Peterson, and many others.

When ordering quantities less than twelve, above titles are $2.95 each.
Not all titles may be available at time of order.

Hearts♥ng Presents
Love Stories
Are Rated G!

That's for godly, gratifying, and of course, great! If you love a thrilling love story but don't appreciate the sordidness of some popular paperback romances, **Heartsong Presents** is for you. In fact, **Heartsong Presents** is the *only inspirational romance book club* featuring love stories where Christian faith is the primary ingredient in a marriage relationship.

Sign up today to receive your first set of four never-before-published Christian romances. Send no money now; you will receive a bill with the first shipment. You may cancel at any time without obligation, and if you aren't completely satisfied with any selection, you may return the books for an immediate refund!

Imagine. . .four new romances every four weeks—two historical, two contemporary—with men and women like you who long to meet the one God has chosen as the love of their lives. . .all for the low price of $9.97 postpaid.

To join, simply complete the coupon below and mail to the address provided. **Heartsong Presents** romances are rated G for another reason: They'll arrive *Godspeed!*

www.heartsongpresents.com